D1524326

I'LL BE GOOD TO YOU
A COMPLETE NOVEL

A Novel By,
CHRISTINE GRAY

Your FACE would

Look better BETWEEN our pages!

Check us out at

www.afterhourspublications.com

CHAPTER ONE
JOHNNY

Same shit. Different day. Nothing changes in the game. People try to steal your shine by talking shit or rape you by sneaking around to reduce your hard work into nothing by catching a glimpse of your work to make it their own. Then there are the females that want to get into your pockets by birthing a whole baby on your ass. After being in this industry, you get into the groove of things quickly, or you're eaten by the wolves to make room for the next motherfucker that's been waiting for you to fall.

I know I might sound sour, but trust me, I ain't. If not for making beats back in the day for my friends, my ass would be toes up, pushing daisies. Shit, the music lab still wasn't enough to keep me out of the man's system. Three years in for ganging and slanging was all it took for both my wannabe black mama and me to see the light. I know this is completely off subject, but why the fuck white chicks that wannabe black all have the same ass look?

See, like the hoes that are strolling naked around in my crib. I glide over the threshold of my house to find that my boy, Rafael has already got the party started. It didn't matter that I could do without all this shit for just one damn night. I swear, I think his punk ass got an issue. Kim K butts, pouty lips, and jet black hair in braids are all I peep. Tan bodies, big tits, and plastic-looking females all stop to welcome me into my own home. Bass being pumped through the speakers, echoes through the house.

I fight to keep a smile on my face when all I want to do is roll my eyes and tell them to get the fuck out. Everyone in the house knows these women could give two shits about the other men. It's my dick; they all want it to be beating down their walls. The thing is, I can take it or leave it. Loose pussy attached to empty-headed women that only want to floss and spend my money is old as fuck. Or maybe, I'm just hungry for one piece of ass in particular.

"Ladies," I chuckle while walking by the group forming around me.

"Nice selection, huh?"

I glance to my left to find Rafael entering the foyer with another woman at his side. You would think after all these years he would have smooth out that crip walk of his, fuckin' fool. Always stunnin', his neck is iced out with gold and diamond necklaces. His shirt is open to show off his chest and tattoos that he says he got while in the gangs, which is bullshit. Nobody dares to call him for the weak shit he is out of fear of pissing me off. At times, I wonder why the hell I never cut his loud mouth self off. I guess I'm just a sucker for the past. I mean, where the fuck is his lazy, slow boat ass is gonna go, if not on my coattails. Not that I haven't encouraged him...even offered up seed money to help him spread his wings. The fucker just wanna be a turd that's stuck on the hair in my ass crack.

He grins, flashing his gem-encrusted silver grill.

"Oh, look bitches and hoes," grumbles Chana, my sister.

Don't let the fact that she seems stuck on age eighteen fool you. She's a full-grown woman that boast one helluva mean left hook. Her mind is like a steel trap. She never misses a beat, and business is her life. That playground nursery rhyme about making a dollar out of 15 cents, I swear was about her ass. After I was lured back to the States to make beats for a few up and coming friends, she's been right at my side... keeping me right and steady. She isn't my only family. She's just the only one that matters.

"Johnny's been in the studio all day, WORKING," she stresses. "He needs to rest."

Now, that's one thing I can't abide, when a female thinks that she's got the right to disrespect my sister. Chana is my do or die, my blood, and the one that will always be on my speed dial, while the one rolling her eyes is nothing but a rolly and not a stop.

"You lost a contact or something?" I ask frowning. "Yeah, you better fix your fuckin' face," I snap.

"Calm down, take a breath," says Rafael as he dislodges himself from his arm candy. "She didn't mean nothing, right?" he presses glancing at the scared girl. "See, all good. Why don't you go get cleaned up and take a hit of this a few times," he offers as he shoves a fat joint in my hand.

I can't even enjoy the craftsmanship put into rolling it because I'm still stabbing the female with my mean gaze, which brings me back to my other rant about these chicks. They can never be as stacked and beautiful as a natural black woman, so embrace what you have and make peace with it. Instead of looking like a clown and a fool trying to twerk what your mama never gave you, come at me with what you have and let's have some fun. Just because I'm called the 'white Luther Vandross', which I don't think I am that good by the way, and hang out with African Americans, Jamaicans, and Puerto Ricans doesn't mean I can't appreciate ALL women. Obviously, Rafael and the world didn't get that memo.

"Nah," I sigh as I pass the joint back to him. "Chana is right. I am tired. I got too much on my mind."

"Which is why I went through all this trouble," promises Raf.

"Have fun, man," I smirk while squeezing his shoulder. I hope the bone-crushing pressure I'm applying and the straight stare I'm giving him is all it takes to let him know, I mean what I say.

"Well, okay," he chuckles weakly.

The females don't even hide their disappointment that it's his dick they'll be entertaining instead of mine, tonight.

"I'm going to need to see ID," announces Chana.

"Who do you-"

"Get your shit and bounce, bitch," I spit. "As a matter of a fact, all ya'll get the fuck out," I snarl.

"B,b,but, but-"

"All you got to do is do as she says," growls Raf. "Everything is on the up and up. See, they're getting their wallets," he rattles.

He comes close to me, "Come on, man, help a brother out," he begs.

I want to list all the things I've done to help his broke down ass out, but I bite my tongue.

"And your cell phones, too," adds Chana.

She places a locked box on the side table for the girls to drop their mobiles in. What goes on in the house stays in the house. I shake Raf loose and head for the stairs. I got to get a grip, though. I mean, I am acting like a douche bag. I claim it's all work and shit, but it's not. It's that goddamn woman. I curse the day my rubbernecking ass peeked her Instagram account. Since that day, I've been like a crack head, stalking her ass and trying to get the hookup. Lord knows I don't want to play the celebrity card to get a date, but for some reason, I know I can't count on that getting me a win.

You know how they say that some men just know which females to try to run game on and which they need not even to try? Well, from what I can see, she isn't about the foolery. Of course, people play all kinda games on social media. They'll catfish your ass into thinking they have millions in the bank and a body of your dreams. Not this woman, though. It's the reason why I can't get her out of my mind because I KNOW all the glitter, she's throwing my way is all gold.

For weeks, I've created fake accounts in hopes of getting her to give me the time of day. Nothing. Her slick mouth cut me down each fuckin' time. Black, mixed, white, Iranian, I've tried hooking her only to fail. Finally, with my wounded pride in hand, I fessed up to my friend who got me on the road in the first place. It was his cell I was glancing over at when I saw the chocolate goddess with the long legs, Thicke thighs, full breast, and a juicy bubble butt. Her confidence is amazing, too. Unlike the women that circulate in my orbit, she handles her own. While many men in my industry want their ladies to be controlled by dollars. Me, I don't give a fuck.

Hitting the landing, I turn left to head for my rooms. I'm reminded of how blessed I am. From a roach-infested hell hole in the Bronx to a 12,000 square foot mansion is mind-boggling. I live in a neighborhood that's so quiet that I have to make noise to keep myself from getting jumpy. For once, I don't have to watch my back. I can open the windows and stand in front of them to watch the life outside without the fear of witnessing a shooting or being shot. The concept is weird as hell, but I'm thankful I made it out.

My cell vibrates in my back, jeans pocket. I pop a damn finger getting it out to read the caller ID.

"Taking your time, huh?" I mumble.

"Who me?"

"Man, save the act. What you got for me?"

"No small talk?"

"Fool, don't make me come for you," I warn.

"But if you hurt me, how am I going to tell you how I just helped you out?"

I slow my steps to stand in the outer room of my bedroom. I swallow hard. I won't lie. I'm excited as fuck. I got butterflies and all that shit.

"What you mean?"

"Well, I called a...friend, and I was able to-"

"Wait! Wait," I demand while making it to the sofa. I'm acting like a crushing bitch, but I don't want to miss a word. For the record, your man will never admit to getting excited over your call or text when you hit him back. Trust me. We aren't that much different from ya'll. We just hide it behind being hard. "Okay, I'm listening."

"I went through some shit, and I'm going to catch so much shit tonight when I get home."

"Yeah, yeah, I'll pay you back. Hold up. You owe me, motherfucker. All the times I covered for you," I remind him in a rush.

"No games, okay... Are you sure you want to do this? It ain't like you don't have pussy on tap. Why you wanna fuck with this one?" he asks, seriously.

For a fact, I shouldn't be jealous of Yosef, but hearing him trying to warn me off of this chick on the low got to me.

"Why? You have a soft spot for her? Is that why you were on her page in the first place?"

Shit, I tried but failed to keep the stank out of my tone.

"You said it right, SOFT because that's all I'll be," he reassures me. "Listen, Tia is a friend of a very, VERY special friend. I don't want to fuck that up. Get me," he explains, slowly.

"Sure, a friend of someone you wanna smash or have smashed. Got it. Now, spill," I grunt.

He sighs. "All I got is she's for sure single, three weeks and counting. She got a teenage daughter. She does play around, but she don't bring men around. Really sassy. I know that from first-hand knowledge. Um, that's all I got."

"Fuck man, I got all that from her IG account," I fume. I see my hopes being dashed.

"Oh, so you been able to get her to converse?"

"No, if I did-"

"Then shut the hell up and let me finish," he snaps.

I grind my teeth. I swear if he wasn't my boy, I'd be all over his head.

"I got you in the door."

I perk up. I mean, I'm wearing a smile that damn near is passing ear to ear. I lick my lips. Straightening up, I lean over to place my elbow on my knee.

"Really?"

Jesus, the excitement in my voice has erased some of its natural bass.

"I was able to get through to her to tell her that I have a rich friend that needs a designer. I told her you'd be popping in her IG to feel her out. You know, see if she makes the cut. She's excited about it."

"Okay, okay, okay," I repeat like an idiot as I try to get my cover story straight. "I'll make sure to keep it all business-like. I won't come on too strong so not to scare her off. Yeah, I know what to do."

I don't know if I'm attempting to convince myself or him. Either way, I'm in the door. Now, I can work my magic to get Tia to... What? No doubt, I want to get a taste of what she is hiding between her thighs. Beyond that, hell if I know. Then again, sexing might be all that it's chalked up to be anyway.

"Thanks, man."

"Welcome. Don't fuck it up and make sure to give her some business. I mean of the paying kind," he adds, knowing exactly where my mind is.

"I will," I chuckle.

When the call ends, nothing can't bug me at the moment. Head down, I quickly make yet another bogus Instagram account as I walk into the bathroom. Checking the time, I debate if I should reach out to her tonight or wait.

10:25, I read.

Yosef's Canadian aunt that took me in, hammered into my head that it was rude to call a female after ten. My thumb hovers over the search magnifying glass to locate her account. Teaching wins out. I don't want to come off as being rude. I'll hit her up early in the morning. Now that I'm this close, I can wait. Gripping my hard dick, I know he feels completely the opposite. For a second, I consider going downstairs to fuck around. Shit, why the hell not? It's not like me and Tia are an item. I am footloose and fancy-free. I'm in need of some good head and some mediocre cunt to hold me over.

I turn on the water, test it, then get in the shower. Going directly under the stream, I relax. I can't help but smile. See, I always get my way. If a hard start in life taught me only one thing, it's persistence in all things. Career, business, family, life, and relationships ...it's the same principle. You may have to step back, conjure up another plan of attack just as long as you keep your ass on the battlefield, you'll win. What does the good book say, "The race isn't given to the fast or strong, but to the one that endures to the end." The thought that I'm not going to fuck Tia never enters my mind. In fact, all I've been envisioning is her fat lips, both sets ingesting my dick.

"A designer," I whisper to myself while washing up.

Already, a plan is formulating to lay the foundation of how I'm going to get Tia in my trap. If she's as empowered as I think she is, then I know she's career focused. Yes, it's all coming together. I can't wait to get out of the shower. I scrub the plush towel over my hair and face before wrapping it around my waist. I exit the bathroom the same way I entered, with cell in hand.

The giggling in my room causes my head to snap up. I'm lost for a few seconds as I wonder what the hell is going on. That's when my eyes land on the pair of women laying in my bed.

RAF, I sigh, mentally.

Funny how you can work yourself up mentally to the point that nothing else seems to satisfy until you get the one thing you're obsessing over. The realization that Tia had become a strong source of my desire hits me like a punch in the gut. I watch the two women riving on the bed with little emotion. Unfortunately, the one-eyed, spitting monster struggling to get a peek from under the towel isn't as committed to the cause as I am. He doesn't even care that one of the women is that disrespectful bitch with the crack whore mouth.

"Move to the rug...by the fireplace," I smirk.

My eyes say, "I can't wait," while my mind is saying, "Yuck."

So, why don't I kick their asses out? Why did I give these two false hope by moving them to the floor? Well, cause I'm a jackass. Plus, I didn't want them grinding, leaking all over my Egyptian Cotton sheets to leave the fabric soaked and smelling of ass mixed with ran through pussy.

"I warned everyone downstairs that I wasn't in the mood," I remind the ladies.

See, I'm not ALL jackass. I already know the answer that I'm going to get.

"You'll change your mind once you see what you're missing," moans the chick with the sleeve tattoo.

Maybe if I hadn't been doing the backstroke in pussy since I was fourteen, what she said might be true, but there was no tempting me. Over the years, a man should have learned a bit of restraint when it comes to sex. It doesn't matter that I'm hard as fuck. I ain't going for a dip.

"Show me," I smile as I slide onto my bed.

A few minutes in, I narrow my eyes. Not because I want to join the fray. Nah, I'm trying to focus my gaze on getting the best view of this chick's eating technique. Ol' crack mouth is teaching me a few tricks. So much, I lean up to make sure I don't miss a stroke of her tongue. Her figure-eight movements have the tattooed woman thrusting her hips in the hope of getting the licker to ease up on her clit to dive between the pink folds that I can see contracting with need.

All is good. My cock is throbbing. I can feel the first droplets of pre-cum squeezing its way through my mushroom-shaped tip. I lick my lips, wondering what her mouth could do for my hard-on. Gripping my balls, I bite back a groan. Then it happened. Like a bucket of cold water, Fate steps in to keep me true to my quest of saving myself for Tia. One...two slender fingers with one-inch nails attached penetrate the woman's body. I physically recoil and my dick drops his head, to tap out. My eyes roam the face of the chick that's getting her flesh poked. I can make out her surprise and a slight change in her excitement. Well, no shit. I mean, I never like watching that bullshit even in porn. How can having pointy nails rammed up your cunt feel good?

SHOWS OVER, I think while patting my retreating dick. BUT THE MAIN EVENT IS COMING.

My promise makes my cock jerk one last time before going completely soft. I smirk at the thought. Going back to my initial task at hand, I scoop up my cell. The time of night isn't a factor when it comes to this. Not when these people have been after me for a while to be apart of what they are doing. Even though their cause is a good one, I wasn't motivated till now to sign up. Hey, I'm a selfish son of a bitch, but whatever.

ME: RUBAN, IF YOU STILL NEED ANOTHER NAME ON THE TICKET I GUESS I AM IN.

Even in the pause, it takes for him to reply, I don't glance up to see what phase the two are in on the floor.

FATBOY: JOKING?

ME: NEVERMIND THEN.

FATBOY: HOLD UP. WAIT A SEC

ME: IT'S TOO FUCKIN LATE TO BE SAYING SOMETHING IF I WAS JOKING, DIP SHIT.

FATBOY: YESS!! THIS IS GONNA BE HUGE

ME: DON'T YELL.

FATBOY: SORRY. FORGOT YOU HATE THAT SHIT.

He must have also forgotten I hate when people text in all lower case, too. Use what you learned in school, people.

FATBOY: NO TAKE BKS. I GOT THIS TEXT. THANKS MAN. THE PAPERWORK WILL BE IN YOUR EMAIL.

The warm feeling I'm experiencing has nothing to do with the good deed I just signed up for. It's actually the warmth of excitement. If only I had another kind of warmth... the moist, tight, gushy stuff to coat my cock and wet my nuts.

"Thanks for the company. Shows over."

I follow up on my statement by switching off the electric fireplace.

"W, um, that was just act one," whispers the tattooed chick.

I let her crawl a few inches across the wooden floor towards me before I break shit down.

"I ain't buying what you are giving," I whisper back.

She freezes to glance over her shoulder to the loudmouth. I roll my eyes. Swinging my legs to the side of the bed, I prepare to get up.

"I haven't cum yet," pouts the rude woman.

"Well, sit on her fuckin face till you do. Get out," I snarl.

Shit, women think that they are the only ones that have to put their foot down when it comes to advancements. Nowadays, hoes are as bold as fuck.

"What, are you gay?" spits the loud chick.

"Shut up. Let's go," mumbles the tatted one while she tugs on her friend's arm. "You'll never have a chance if you-"

"Fuck JOHNNY THICKE," spits the other woman, putting extra stress on my name.

I shrug my shoulders. That salt in her wounds must be burning. To put the last nail in the coffin, I stand to reveal my lower half. Licking my lips, I grip my sleeping unit to pump it. Both women stumble during their retreat. Eyes wide, they take in the sight of my pipe that's not even fully hard. The size is still enough to make them either thank God it's not destroying their guts or out of lust to take a ride. I chuckle at their reaction.

Whatever. I'm finally alone. To make sure it stays that way, I press a button to engage the automatic locks on the door to my suite. No drama, tonight. Unlike other nights, my mind isn't plagued with beats, lyrics, or tour dates. Actually, I can feel the first peaceful sleep I've had in a long time coming on. The Tia effect is some shit, huh?

**

MORNING

"What the fuck?"

Turning in time to catch the odd look on Chana's face, I don't wonder the reason behind it. Her head darts from side to side. She's probably wondering if she's walked into the *Twilight Zone* to see me up.

"Is the house cleaned?" I ask, ignoring her antics.

"Um, yeah. You're dressed."

Not a question. She's just stating the obvious.

"Yes, right after I brushed my teeth and wiped my ass after a shit," I laugh.

My happiness so early is making her wary.

"I need the name of the girl you fucked last night. I want to send her a token of appreciation."

I raise my hand, palm facing her. "No need for gifts, but if you want to tell my hand, thank you, be my guest," I tease.

Chana roams me from head to toe.

"Shit! What you took, Johnny? Hand the shit over now!" she fumes.

Hand out, she eats up the ground to glare at me.

"I swear I'm clean, Chana. I'm high on life...nothing else," I promise, slowly.

Leaning over into her searching eyes, I open my eyes wide to allow her to examine my blue-green orbs.

"Holy Father," she says in disbelief while stepping back. "I'm sorry. You're just so, so...put together," she explains.

"Well, good morning to you, too, sis," I smile.

"Going to tell me why?"

"In a few, but right now, we need to get moving."

"Right," she remarks with a clap.

I watch her from the corner of my eye when I hook my finger in the sports coat she must have overlooked hanging on the back of a chair. She works her mouth, trying to decide if she should ask. My seemingly lack of attention to her causes her to drop it. Instead, she goes into our routine.

"You have a 9 am with the property manager at the estate in Greenwich Village. Are you still putting it on the market?"

"I might hold it till the new year."

"Okay, well you have an hour to decide. After that, you have back to back with a few promoters that want you on their fall festival line up. Then, a photo shot for GQ."

"What time is the shoot?" I question as I make a move to leave the rooms.

Chana, standing at 5'8" has no problem keeping up with my 6'2", wide strides. She double-checks her tablet before answering.

"12:15."

"Alright, while I'm showing off my resting bitch face, I need you to take a meeting for me," I inform her.

"Meeting? What kind of meeting?"

"Is Rafael still lingering?" I question, not replying.

"I, I don't think so," she stutters.

"Go, make sure," I instruct while gliding down the stairs. "If he's still here, kick him out. He has a goddamn house. I'm tired of hosting his parties and playing wingman. He needs to step up his player's game. Tell Hammer to change the codes at the gate, the locks on the doors, and no he can't be let on the property."

Chana's hand bites into my arm to pull me to a stop.

Tilting her head, she stares at me.

"What the fuck is going on...really?"

Patting the side of her face, I take a deep breath. "Shit happens, minds change...now, hurry up," I command with a shove to send her on the way.

She walks away, still looking in my direction. Then rights herself to quicken her steps down the hallway.

THAT'S RIGHT, ...RUN ALONG.

Leaning against the wall, I finally do what I've been counting the hours and seconds till this moment in time. I bite my lips and swipe up on my cell. It comes alive to open the IG app. Since I've planned out my words, my fingers fly across the keyboard.

ME: GOOD MORNING. I BELIEVE THIS IS TIA SYMONE'S ACCOUNT. YOU SHOULD HAVE BEEN GIVEN THE HEADS UP THAT I WOULD BE CONTACTING YOU TO CONTRACT YOUR

DESIGNING SERVICES. I CAN'T ELABORATE AT THIS MOMENT WHY I AM SEEKING A DESIGNER. WHAT I AM FREE TO SAY IS THAT THIS IS A LIFE-CHANGING OPPORTUNITY FOR YOU AND YOUR BUSINESS. I HAVE TO SECURE AN EXPERIENCED INTERIOR DESIGNER, ASAP, SO FORGIVE ME IF I'M COMING OFF RUDE. I CAN'T DO FACE TO FACE, BUT MY MANAGER CAN BREAK AWAY TO MEET WITH YOU BETWEEN NOON AND 1 PM TODAY. LET ME KNOW IF YOU ARE AVAILABLE WITHIN THAT TIME FRAME? YOSEF SPOKE HIGHLY OF YOU. IF THERE IS A WAY TO OPEN THE DOOR FOR A FRIEND OF A FRIEND, I WOULD PREFER IT. TILL LATER.

Shocked, huh? I write songs for A-listers. I create raps that's not for the playground, but the college lecture halls. Upstairs are volumes of dictionaries I've committed to memory and my library is full of first edition classics. What I'm saying is not to take my tattooed self at face value. There are layers, chapters to my book. Oh, I can talk the street shit. I'll never be rid of those habits, but I've graduated from it. I wanted more, so I worked for it. No need to hustle to make it out only to still linger in the life that you fought so hard to rise above.

In my garage, you'll find two cars. I'm not holding down a car lot. The limo I ride in is from a car service business I invested in. That's why I have the same driver. The private jet is a rental through a friend that rents it out to make money off of the plane. I'm not wasting my money on that bullshit. You won't see me iced out, but that don't mean I don't own it. I have two hidden safes full of gold coins, cut diamonds, and other gems. My property portfolio will have you snatching your edges. To finish out my investments, are paintings, investments in weed farms, startups, and blocks of buildings. Yeah, I listened to Jay-Z's, THE STORY OF OJ. The dude was spitting wisdom that so many haven't grabbed hold to, yet.

"We're going to be late."

Chana's declaration snaps my eyes off my cell. I calm myself over the fact that Tia hasn't responded, yet. Opening the door, I step to the side for Chana to exit first. The back door to a black Bentley is standing open for her. She thanks Richey as she slides in. Heading to the opposite, back door, I nod my head towards Richey before I get in.

It takes everything within me not to turn into a crushing bitch at the vibrations of my cell. My heartbeat is in my ears. I fight to keep my face free of feelings as I read.

CREATIVESPACES: GOOD MORNING. YES, I WAS INFORMED THAT YOU MIGHT REACH OUT TO ME FOR YOUR DESIGNING NEEDS. A SECRET PROJECT? I'M VERY INTERESTED TO HEAR MORE. ALTHOUGH YOUR TIME FRAME IS PUTTING ME IN A BIT OF A BIND, MY NOSINESS TO KNOW WHAT YOU'RE SEEKING HAS ENCOURAGED ME TO MAKE MYSELF AVAILABLE TO YOUR MANAGER. I WILL BE EXPECTING YOUR MANAGER NO LATER THAN 12:05. AFTER THAT TIME, I WILL HAVE TO DECLINE THE PROJECT. OFFICE DETAILS ARE IN MY BIO.

BEST REGARDS.

I re-read the message. My silence in the car causes tension to enter the space. From flattery to serving me my ass with a sweet smile, and correct punctuation is what I pick up between the lines. My hand tightens involuntarily on my cell.

"Are you alright, sir?"

My gaze moves to connect with Richey's in the rearview mirror. I swallow down the stream of curses I want to spew. No doubt how I'm grinding my teeth, and the flexing of my jaw indicates my level of piss. How the fuck this woman is going to come at me like this after my nice message?

"Hey," says Chana with an elbow to my arm.

"Yeah, I'm fine...peachy," I grunt. I loosen my grip on the phone. "That meeting, you need to be on time." Stiff jaw, the sentence comes out in a growl.

Chana slowly clicks on her tablet. "Okay, details; who, what, you know."

"It's a designer for the Greenwich house."

Upset, Chana tosses the tablet on the floor of the car. "I'm sick of asking. I ain't gonna beg, so what the fuck is up," she yells.

Close to my heart, my little sis is the reason why I do the shit I do. She's the only one that can get away with talking to me in such a way, but even she knows the time and place to show her ass.

"Why you got to get crazy?" I tease to lighten the mood. "Listen, I got tired of Fatb-"

"Don't call him that," she remarks. "The man's lost over 60 pounds."

"Sorry, um, Ruban...I got tired of him hitting me up, so I said I'd do his celebrity contest."

"Really?"

The word is spoken in unison between Chana and Richey. They need to watch it. Speaking in time like that is a dead giveaway.

"Yes. Don't look at me like that. It is for a good cause, after all," I snip.

"Uhuh...and what is that cause?"

I shift in the leather seat. Fuck! What is the cause? I didn't think that far ahead. Autism? Nah, I'm sure that one is already taken. Shit!

"Well, that's for you to decide. I want something that will give back to an impoverished community...like after school program, school tech, or maybe to fix up some houses."

Chana stares at me for a few seconds. I can fake it with others, but not her. The little smirk tugging on the corner of her lips tells me she isn't buying it.

"Should I interview possible designers. I can call who did our house," she offers.

"No, that wouldn't be fair. Anyway, I think it's for up and coming to get some spotlight. The meeting is with somebody that Yosef knows."

She nods her head. Picking up the tablet, "What's the name?"

"I don't have all of that." The lie passes smoothly over my gums. "The place is called, Creative Designs," pausing I dig a Sticky Note from my pocket. "This is the address. The owner knows you are coming. Do not tell the designer who I am. I don't want stuff leaking."

"Leaking?"

"Yes, leaking...people talk. I want to have the chance of finding a good designer without the big name ones knocking at my door." Damn, I'm good at this lying shit.

"Alright," she remarks while reading the note. "This is good, Johnny. I've been trying to get you to show a little bit of yourself to the public," she smiles.

I smile back. What I want to show isn't for the public. It's for Tia...and Tia alone.

CHAPTER TWO
CHANA

"Johnny is full of shit."

Richey cuts his eyes in my direction.

"Oh, come on...you don't believe all that bull, do you?"

Richey, always the cautious one doesn't reply. It didn't matter that he ran the streets with Johnny back in the day, or the fact that he and his Ma looked after me whenever my Mother brought a new guy home to stay. He still didn't cross the line of boss and employee. He treated Johnny like the man that signed his checks and kept his opinions to himself. I guess that's a good thing, until times like this when I want someone to bitch with.

"He's helping out a friend."

I roll my eyes so hard I almost stumble on the sidewalk. Don't get me wrong. My brother would give you his shirt off his back. He's good like that, but he's also the kind that's watching, even when you think he isn't. It only takes him seeing you backstabbing, cheating, or doing something wrong for him to write you off. He'll work with you, yeah. He just won't be down with you. People see him as a product of the streets. The tattoos inking him from neck to ankle gave people the wrong thoughts about him. He's the bad boy, the trailer park white trash that grew up in the projects with the 'make you cum' voice.

That's why I've been after him for so long to let the World glimpse the man who believes in blessing in secret to be rewarded in the light. He might let talk and shit roll off his shoulders, but not me. I take names. I save dates and times. I plot and wait to pay each fucker back.

"Oh," I shout when I remember something. "And he's putting a stop to Rafael coming around." I pause to watch Richey's reaction. "See, Whatcha say to that?" I ask as I wave my hand wildly.

This piece of info makes Richey slow his steps in thought. I can see he wants to weigh in but sticks to his guns.

"You're going to be late," he finally speaks.

Placing a hand on my lower back, he rushes me down the sidewalk, through the double doors, and onto the elevator. I bite my lip in frustration. He's right; I know. I just don't want to hear it. It would only take him bitching out my brother one time, and I'm going to be all up in his ass. It wouldn't matter that I asked, or that I instigated it. I can talk shit, but you better not about my family.

The chime of the elevator alerts me; It's time to get out of my head. If Johnny is serious about doing this designing thing, I need to ensure he isn't put to shame. I'll tell you this; If the waiting room of Creative Designs is a sign of talent, this designer has it in spades. I take my time examining the area. The space is small, but shit if the person didn't use it to make a powerful first impression. Making use of the old, dark wood paneling on the walls, the person created a rich room that boasts undertones of an Old English home while adding accents of African art and appeal. It brought to mind those shows where the people showcased their family paintings of those dead and gone while showing off the things they brought back from their Kenya vacation. Even though the room felt high class and expensive to appeal to that level of client, the room was still welcoming and warm with comfortable seating. Soothing jazz streamed into the room from hidden speakers. The high, brimstone windows shined a bright light in to soften up the appearance of the area.

"Are these curtains?" I question in awe as I walk over to examine the fabric myself.

"No, well they are now, but they were actually old tapestries found at an estate sale," answers the receptionist. "They aren't worth anything if you're worried about that."

"Of course," I mumble. "It's an excellent use of repurposing," I praise. "It ties the room together very well, too," I add.

"I have to agree. Many people are enthralled with the African folklore sown into the fabric."

"I bet," I whisper. "I have a meeting with the owner on behalf of my employer," I say, coming to my wits.

I take a spin around the reception room while the employee goes back behind the desk to place a call.

"That's a man."

Richey's hissed statement has my jaw dropping. As nonchalant as I can, I steal a look.

"No," I remark.

"The hands," he says with a slight jerk of his head. "Good work, but the hands tell it."

"It won't be long now. Can I offer you something? Water? Hot tea?"

I'm too busy trying to see through the beauty of caramel-colored wom... er... person that there's a delay in my response. I open my mouth to reply only to be knocked off my ass.

"Hello, I'm Tia Symone."

I normally give a stiff handshake, but the surprise causes my hand to go limp.

"Y, yes, nice to meet you," I chuckle, weakly. "I'm Chana."

"This way, please," instructs Tia while she waves us towards a hallway. She glances at her watch. "I had to fit you in, so please forgive me. Oh, were you offered refreshments?"

"We were," chimes in Richey, saving my ass in hopes of giving me a moment to recover. "Tea for her, water for me, please," he beams at the person that for sure is one helluva pretty trans.

"Wonderful, this way, then. Thank you, Ryann," Tia tosses over her shoulder. "Second door to your left."

"Another perfect room," I gush while taking a seat.

"Well, thank you. When you're a designer, every bit of space is an open canvas to create."

Her smile flashes perfect pearly whites. Now, in the past, I'll admit there have been women and girls that produced a bit of heat within me whenever I saw them or were around them. This, this woman here is creating a bright flame that I can't seem to look away from. I mean fuckin' perfect in every goddamn way. She has to have had work. Of course, I'm saying that to ease my longing to switch places with her. I would so bodysnatch her shell to gladly live out my remaining days. Tia has the kind of dark, chocolate skin that glows and appears to be brushed onto flesh. Large almond-shaped eyes with long lashes. I don't know if they are fake because they are so natural looking. Full lips are colored, but not bright to bring attention to something that is so perfectly shaped; you can't help but follow them when she speaks. High cheekbones, long, regal neck, then comes a curvaceous body that just won't quit, with long, Thicke legs to finish it off. I send up a prayer in hopes that at least her feet are ugly.

"How can I be of service?"

Her question creates a chain reaction in my mind. A smile slowly forms on my lips.

Now I see.

Johnny's lies don't hold up in the light of this new knowledge.

"First off, thank you for taking my appointment at such short notice. I'll get right to it. My employer requires a designer. You would be commissioned to create multiple rooms in the hope of both you and him winning the celebrity reality show, Celebrity Devine Design. Have you heard of it?"

TIA

This woman is going to have to forgive me for the awkward stare on my face. My eyes are bulging while I look as if she's just sprouted two heads. Do I know the show? The question is almost laughable. Of course, I know about the goddamn show. Oh, my fucking lord! This isn't happening to me. There is a person that wants me, me to lead up their team in an attempt to not only win the title of season two but also a million dollars to the designer along with a spread in Architectural Digest. That title will set my business up.

I'm a fake. Well, let me explain that. I am a designer, a damn good one, but a soon to be broke one. Old Uncle Sam came a knocking to collect on my student loans. I have a teenage daughter that I'm trying to care for, while my mother does nothing but talk bullshit. I'm hemorrhaging money to keep up this façade of being great. I learned long ago, for the clients I want to net, I have to give off the illusion that I'm able to meet their expensive taste…to a degree. They don't want a basement operating designer, and I really don't want to work for a customer that can't open the doors and pay me my worth.

"Yes, I'm aware of the show. I watched it actually, but I thought it wasn't going to return for a second season," I answer, at last.

"That might be so, but with my employer deciding to sign on, let's just say the network is ready to get to taping."

I arch my eyebrow. "And who is your employer."

"He desires to remain in the dark until a designer is found, and the contract is signed. I will say that he is a top-selling singer, producer, and songwriter."

Fuck, that can be anyone.

"Not knowing makes things very difficult, but I understand. He doesn't want to get anyone's hopes up. Well," I pause to think. "How about we chat. I 'll be happy to show you some of my work, then we'll go from there," I suggest.

"Perfect."

Where the hell is Ryann with the drinks? His slow ass is probably worried about chipping a nail. I get to my feet, "Let's move over here. It will make viewing the books easier."

I have on my confident smile when I'm shaking in my boots. Thankfully, I applied a double dose of *Degree* just encase I was meeting a heavy hitter, today. We're halfway through the first scrapbook before Ryann appears.

"You have a talent that couldn't have all come from the classroom."

"Thank you," I beam.

Chana knows her shit. She plays dumb to get you in that spot of ease, but she's watching and listening to every word. While some may dismiss her for not having what the masses considered beauty, she's nothing but. Olive colored skin tone, a bit on the lanky, tall side, then you notice her Thicke, wavy black hair, freckles, and a Barbra Streisand nose that I find really cute.

"Thank you," she looks up from the book to take her tea. "Um, I think I've seen enough."

I make sure to steady my hand when I remove the scrapbook album from her legs. Never let them see you hungry. I say that, but I'm already mentally preparing a speech to beg for a chance.

"Great! I'll give you a couple of days to discuss things with-"

"No need. I've been authorized to offer you a contract if I liked what I saw...and I like what I see. You can draw it up, sign it, and he will return it back to you this evening. He's requesting to meet with whomever I pick, this evening over dinner. Taping starts in a matter of days. Will that be a problem?"

"At such short notice," I mumble. I let the silence into the room as if I'm worried about Brittany knowing damn well my Mama lives with us. "I'll make a few calls, but sure."

Chana holds up her hand, "I know you said you've seen the show, but let me say a few things, okay. This is reality T.V., which means there will be drama. Add the desire to win, and you damn sure know there will be a lot. I you to be aware this is a two month commitment."

"I'm not worried about that. I can give it as good as it's given with class and a smile," I interject.

"For some reason, I know you can," she beams. "Also, you will be a team...working together. I'll tell you now, he likes to win."

No duh, so do I, I nod.

"Also, there will be cameras, following you, in your face, you understand me?"

"I understand," I nod.

"Wonderful. Well, if you can get the contract, we'll get this dream team formed," she laughs.

You don't have to ask me twice. I slide from the expensive chair that I'm still making monthly payments on to head for my desk. This is the time when the small talk enters the room. It's all the normal topics. How did you get into design? Where did you study? What is your list of clients? I keep up the chatter while I start up my computer to generate the contract. I have to force my fingers and my brain to remain engaged when all I want to do is get these people the hell out so I can jump, shout, and call my Mom to tell her the news.

"Make sure to send Yosef a gift basket."

I chuckle at Chana's comment. "Oh, I for sure owe him a solid."

"How did you two meet?" She asks.

I don't slow my pace while I answer. "I tutored him years ago."

"Oh, really? You went to Eleanor Roosevelt High? We did, too?" Chana informs me a bit excited.

"No, no, I met Yosef at Castle Hill Middle. I needed a job after graduating. I still helped him out when he was in high school, too," I trail off into a mumble as I concentrate on making sure the verbiage is all correct in the document.

CHANA

I'm having a hard time closing my mouth. For her to have tutored Yosef in middle school would mean she's way, way older than what she looks. Glancing to my left, I do a double-take at the college diploma on the wall.

"Hey, what does that say? The date? What's the date?" I whisper in a rush while tapping Richey's leg. He's much closer to the frame on the wall than I am.

"Class of 2004."

Okay, that narrows it down a little, but not enough. I tap my painted finger on my leg. I got it.

"It's a good thing you were able to help him out. Lord, knows I could have used some of that. Did you go to Roosevelt? If so, were you there when Coach Mitch was there?"

"Old handsy Mitch," I huff. "Yeah, I was there. Actually, it was my senior year when he was caught in the locker room with that girl giving him sloppy head. Oh, please excuse me."

I wave off her break from business attitude. Tia could have said Dumbo flew by the window, and I wouldn't have cared. I wait until she turns her head back to her laptop before I shake Richey's arm frantically.

"She's-"

"I know."

"No, she's-"

"Shut up," he whispers, jerking his arm away.

"TEN YEARS older than-"

"Alright, here you go."

Tia's announcement causes us to break apart as if we weren't just talking about her. I stand to approach her elegant desk while the printer located on the shelf behind her spits out the pieces of paper.

"I'm signing my portion now."

I watch her hand glide over the signature line indicated for her name to leave a flowing, flowery signature. I take that moment to marvel over her body, her hands, her lowered head once again. Damn, the woman didn't age one fucking bit. She can very easily pull off being in her early to mid-twenties.

"Here you are."

"Thank you," I beam. "I'm sure it will be signed before your evening meeting."

"Great. Am I to be still kept in the dark as to who I'll be working with?"

"Oh, I'm not going to ruin the surprise...and I'm calling Yosef, so don't try to pry it out of him," I tease. Reaching out my hand, I'm in a much better mental space to give her a firm shake. "It's going to be so much fun working with you."

I'm not lying, either. I'm damn near giddy thinking about it. My brother has met his match.

TIA

I stand transfixed long after the door to the reception room is closed. I count until about 13 before I let out a scream of excitement.

"You did it."

"I did it!" I repeat in a shout.

Like kids, Ryann and I jump up and down with clasped hands.

"Hold my mule. I'm going to shout right here," I say, repeating a line from Pastor Sherly Ceasar.

"Ryann held out his arm for support for me as I do my Holy Ghost dance in place.

"Praise Him! Praise Him! Go gurl," he sings.

Out of breath, I stop. "We better stop playing like this, but thank You Jesus," I shout.

"Okay, okay, what's the job?" He presses.

"Weren't you listening at the door?" I wonder.

"Nah, I got a call on my cell," he huffs, rolling his pretty contact eyes.

"Well, you'll never believe it."

"If you told me, I just might fuckin' will," he sasses.

"It's a spot on that designer reality show."

His mouth falls to hang gaping. "Bitch, you lying."

"No, hoe I ain't."

Ryann stumbles back to flop into one of the waiting room chairs.

"That, that show that comes on the E Channel? The one with that good-looking Spanish guy...that show?" He questions while waving his hand in the air.

"Yes, YES, Celebrity Devine Design," I reply in a rush of excitement.

Ryann's eyes bulge as he works his slack mouth, but no words, just sounds of disbelief are coming out.

"Yes, Boo- Kitty...I know right," I beam.

"You know what this means for you?"

"What it means for *us*," I correct him as I wag my finger between us. "It means that we are going to be on TV. It means that we will be working with and meeting famous people. It means that we are going to bleed this for all it's worth, and we're going to make a name for ourselves."

"That's right mama," remarks Ryann in only a way a dramatic trans can. "We are going to Cardi B the shit out of the opportunity. Not only are we going to win, but we are going to be flaming bright. So, who's the celebrity we're teaming up with?"

I shrug. "Hell, if I know, and who gives a fuck. I'll let you know after I have dinner with the guy tonight."

"True dat. Wait, so it's a guy. Oh, gurl! What if you can work that shit and make some kinda love connection," he comments while getting to his feet. His level of excitement just raised to a new height.

"Boy, get the hell out of here with that crap," I frown. "I'm not even entertaining that thought. I'm just focusing on the exposure and winning," I inform him.

"You're right. You're right. No need to give your candy off the shelves when we need to be focusing on securing the store."

"Now, you're thinking. What I look like fucking whoever this guy is and lose out on this opportunity of really establishing this business?" I explain.

"We're on the same page," he promises. "Now, I need to make sure our clothes and hair are on point.

"You do that. I'm cutting out early to go home," I say as I jog towards my office down the hall. "I can't wait to tell Mama and Brit," I shout to make sure my words reach him.

I don't have to tell Ryann to get his shit and leave. I can already hear him opening and slamming drawers. I have full confidence in his ability to have us camera ready. No doubt he's going to bless a few of his close friends by asking them to create designer outfits for us to wear. On the first day of filming, he will have pulled together a hair and makeup team, too. This is a come up for not just he and I, but for everyone that's had our back since day one. Once the door has been opened, it will be up to each and every one of them to make connections of their own.

"Alright, I'm out," I bellow as I head for the exit.

"Okay, oh, ah what put them on your scent, anyway?"

His question causes me to lean back into the office.

"Yosef," I chuckle before walking out to allow the door to close behind me.

CHAPTER THREE
JOHNNY

I'm about to pull my hair out. For the last hour, Fatbo-excuse me, Ruban has been closer than my own shadow. Seems that the network had been on the fence about green lighting season 2, but it's all steam ahead if he can get me to sign on. Needless to say, he's going to be up my ass till he gets the contract as proof for the network that he isn't full of shit.

"Chana!" I sigh in relief. Coming out of the makeup artist chair. "Here she is," I point out to Ruban.

"Please tell me you found a designer," cries Ruban.

"I sure did," smiles Chana.

Don't think I don't notice the slickness tied to her smile. She's holding her tongue. Going into her genuine leather bag, she produces, and hands over the stapled papers.

"Man, if you don't step the hell back," I grumble as I rub my neck in hopes of removing the heat of his breath.

"S-sorry," Ruban mumbles while shifting his weight on his feet. "So, um...are you going to sign?"

"I have no doubt he will," smirks Chana.

I ignore my sister to take the pen Ruban is shoving in my face. Giving me his back, I press on it to sign Tia's contract. Quickly, he produces the network's contract. I put my chicken scratch on that one, too.

"Yes, oh my God, man! You have saved my ass and the asses of so many people needing a paycheck. Thank you." He pauses to think twice about bear hugging me. "Yes, right so, I'll get your filming schedule over to the director."

With a spring in his step, he leaves me with Chana with her shit-eating grin. I wait till I turn away to roll my eyes. I know it's coming.

"So, the designer checked out?"

"Oh, you mean Tia," she mocks. "Checked out as a designer or your next booty call?"

I ease myself into the chair. "What was your impression?"

Chana doesn't answer until she's leaning back against the pop-up styling table with the huge mirror and bright lights.

"Tia is an amazing designer. I really think, no, I *know* you're going to give the others on the show a run for the money."

"That's what I wanted to hear," I say with enthusiasm while getting to my feet.

Chana steps in front of me. "But," she stresses while holding up her hand to block me from moving way.

Sighing, I sit back down.

"As a fuck and suck, no. She's not the one."

I arch my eyebrow. "Not to say that's my plan, but why not?"

She scoffs. "Please, John. It's me you're talking to, but if you wanna play dumb, go ahead."

"I don't have all day to draw this out. You got something to say, say it," I order.

"I think I just did. Tia is not the one. Period."

"Why?" My question comes out a little more forceful than I wanted.

"Because she's a lot more than you can handle."

Oh, shit. Chana just stepped in it. Scooting to the edge of the uncomfortable chair, we're no longer talking like boss and manager. We're getting ready to scrap like sister and brother.

"What that's supposed to mean?"

"What it means is she's got a kid."

The tension that was building in me eases up a bit. "I'm not looking for a wife."

"And that's what I'm trying to say. Tia isn't a plaything."

"You don't know what you're talking about. She's fucked around," I tell her.

"Hell, everyone needs their tires rotated every now and then. Who cares, but that's a whole lot of woman," she warns.

"You think I can't handle her," I chuckle. "Man, she must have made one helluva impression on you."

"Listen, she has her crap together, at least I think she does. Anyway, this is a great opportunity for her. I don't think she gonna munk it up with fucking with you. That isn't a dumb chick riding your jock. She's a full-grown woman," she explains.

"It's just a little fun, Chana. Tia gets something. I'll get something. Hell, even Ruban and whatever charity my winnings will go to will get something. We all fuckin' win at the end of the day."

Chana shakes her head, sickeningly. "You're one low down, dirty, dried-up piece of shit," she growls. "You remember when you were hell-bent on catching that dumb fish? You wasted weeks out on that fish creek. Then when you finally got it on the hook, you couldn't reel it in."

I chuckle while rubbing my chin. Licking my lips, "I won't have a problem getting Tia on my pole," I whisper with a wink.

"Whatever you say, but just like with that fish, you hooked it then you didn't know what the hell to do. You lost your pole, ended up being out of 12 dollars worth of bait, and your pride hurt."

"Thanks for your input," I reply with a smirk.

Chana tosses her hands up in the air. A huge smile causes her face to shine. "No sweat off my back. I just don't want you to come crying to me and asking why I didn't try to cock block you. Either way, I'm going to enjoy watching everything go down from my front row seat."

"Well, you won't be able to see how *everything* goes down," I tease.

**

Honestly, I don't know what I did for the rest of the day. What I do remember is wasting my time in the studio because all I could think about was meeting Tia tonight. Italian, seafood, Japanese...hell, if I couldn't think of something. Mapping out the location of her offices, I can only assume she lives near it. That narrowed down my choices.

Me: *Congrats on getting the contract. How is Daniel? It's a French restaurant on 60 E 65th street.*

Tia: *I know it. 7:15? Thank you, by the way.*

Me: *I'll be there, and you're welcome.*

I'm not too much of a fan, but it's definitely a place to impress. The four-course meals start at $158 for small ass portions of food that will guarantee your ass will be hungry when you leave. The restaurant's saving grace in my eyes is their wine cellar and the intimate lounge eating upper area.

As I look at the onward traffic while I wait to turn into the valet spot, I catch a glimpse of Tia. I lean up in the driver's seat to rubberneck to watch her stroll up the walkway before disappearing through the turn style, gold-plated door. Stepping on the gas, I dart out in traffic to roll up. My door is open before the man can reach my side of the car. When he sees me, he instantly stops in his tracks to gawk. He isn't the only one. From the others outside to those standing within the foyer, people eyes bulge to stare.

I don't care. All my attention is on the woman that's been shuffled to the side to wait for the employees behind the tall, dark wood podium to acknowledge her. I hold my breath for the moment she'll glance up from her cell in wonder of what all the whispering was about. Luckily, it doesn't take too long. Time stills for a second. I know that sounds like a bitch comment, but I won't lie. I'm stunned to finally have the force of her eyes on me. Her eyes widen upon recognizing who I am, then they go cold before she glances away.

Was all that because she's trying to play off being excited? Or does she not like me? I read the movements of her lips; *Jesus don't let it be this fool.*

I frown. Who the fuck she thinks I am?

"Sir, Mr. Thicke."

I break my gaze to glare at the man behind the desk.

"Good evening. Your table is ready," he announces with a wide sweep of his hand.

"I don't want to skip anyone."

"No worries, Sir. Someone called ahead to reserve your table."

He speaks loud enough for the others waiting to hear.

"Thank you. Oh, I have a guest joining me...a Tia-"

"Shit."

Frowning, I turn to look in the direction of the whispered curse. She sheepishly excuses her way to the front of the wannabe diners.

"Good evening, I'm Tia...Tia Symone."

I'm torn between smiling or acting like a cold douche due to her first reaction towards me. Call me petty. I go with the cold. I scan her from head to toe, making her outstretched hand dangle in the air before I give it a shake.

"My guest seems to be here," I address the man instead of speaking to Tia.

The guy nods and gestures for us to follow him. My upbringing, not from my Ma keeps me from walking ahead of her. Actually, I'm gifted with the sight of her ass swaying very nicely, thanks to her high heels.

"Thank you," I mumble.

I allow him to hold out her chair while I take position on my own. Daniel's restaurant is a large one with many dining areas on the lower and upper levels. The ones were placed in only holds ten tables to give off a very quiet setting.

"Have we met before?"

Taken back, Tia bats her eyelids.

"No, I don't-"

"Then what was your reaction towards me all about?"

Her jaw hangs open for a heartbeat. She shifts in her seat, nervously.

"I was just shocked to know that I was here to meet you. Your manager hinted off it was someone in the music industry. I just didn't peg you as a person to sign up for this kind of show."

Leaning back in my chair, I stare at her silently. I'm not upset for the record. I just want her to think about her rudeness for a moment.

"My apologies," she smiles.

All I do is nod. Dropping my eyes to the tablecloth, I got to get my shit together. Her smile has the zipper on my pants straining under my instant hard-on.

"Chana speaks very highly of your work. I really hope what you think about me isn't going to be a problem." I hold my tattooed hand to stop her from talking. "You said sorry, and I accepted. We can move on."

"Thank you," she sighs.

At the pause in our conversation, the waitress makes her way to our table. She introduces herself, hands us the menus while telling us the night's specials, and retreats after taking our drink orders.

"I am really excited for this opportunity. When Yosef asked if I would be open to try out, I thought he was joking around."

"I get why you were knocked on your ass. I've never done anything like this before," I admit.

"So why do it?"

I lick my lips. "I'm doing it for a friend. The guy has put all his money into pitching the show. The network wasn't going to sign on for a season two without a big name on the ticket."

Fuck. I didn't mean to, but after hearing it in the open, I'm coming off a bit arrogant. I can see that feeling cross her pretty face before she hides it.

"I guess he and I have you to thank, then," she smirks.

The chick returning with a bottle of wine gives me the escape I need to keep me from drowning. This dinner isn't going like I dreamed.

"I'm the one thanking my lucky stars. I would have been up the creek without a paddle without Yosef. You're my ace," I praise while tipping my glass in her direction.

Yes, that got me the reaction I needed. After a few glasses, she'll loosen up, I think.

"Don't get too lax, now. I'm sure the others in the contest will be just as good as me."

"But not better," I press.

Now, who's being arrogant? She just tooted her own horn. Shit, don't think about her mouth doing anything other than drinking and eating, I warn myself.

"How do you know him?" She asks.

See, this is the type of mood I wanted to create. Just a date where she and I can get to know each other.

"His mother lived in the same project housing as my family and me. Then when I was in trouble, his mom worked it out for me to live with her sister in Canada."

"Wow, I had heard a little bit about that, but you never know what to believe," she whispers.

"Half the stuff is all lies, but if it gets those sites the clickbait they need to keep people on their payroll..." I trail off with a shrug.

Fifteen minutes flies by and I know I'm failing. She's polite, giving me that fake smile of hers, but the vibe she's giving off, I don't like. It's as if she's taking issue with me over shit that I'm clueless about. I try to make the conversation about her and less about me, but even that isn't working.

"Are you liking the food?" I ask.

Shit, now how can a simple question like that gain me a stiff side-eye? Annoyed, I lean back in my chair.

"The food is great...a little more than I could afford. Thank you for picking this restaurant."

I catch her smirk behind the rim of her wine glass. Is she giving me the cold shoulder because I'm successful? What the fuck is wrong with this woman? Does she want a broke down man that wants to be kept so she can run things? Nah, that can't be it.

"Would you mind telling me a bit about how the reality show works?"

I know she likes to flex her skills. Maybe this will put me in a better light. She raises an eyebrow.

"You've never watched the show?"

"To be honest, I' don't watch a lot of TV at all. When I do, it's a documentary or a classic from the 80's or later," I reply.

"Oh," she nods.

Is that a good nod? Or a fucking idiot nod? One thing I do know is I'm getting tired of trying to figure shit out.

"Well, the show is set up like any reality, contest show. Each week we're given a decorating task. Like, um, they might have us decorate a woman's nursery or a themed roomed of some kind. We're given the rules like, um, we have to use a budget of $200, we're dropped off at a thrift store with only 30 minutes to grab whatever we need. Stuff like that."

"So, we're not decorating just rooms in my house?" I wonder, a bit confused.

"No. They usually move us off location for a few jobs."

"And the people that we do the jobs for; are they voting, or is it the same judges?"

She shrugs. "I've seen episodes that went with the guest people weighing in, and those comments are considered by the judges. Other ways were one of the people actually sat on the panel to cast a vote. Also, they...the judges are always watching. Or the editing makes it seem as if they are watching," she says.

"I see," I grumble.

I've been duked. Fatboy, yeah I'm back to calling him that because I'm pissed, didn't tell me half of this shit. This is going to be a lot more time consuming than I thought.

"I can tell by your sour face that you aren't feeling this," she huffs.

I don't hide my annoyance with her when it flashes in my eyes.

"Let me guess, you thought it was going to be a cameo stop? You know, you pop in, smile for the cameras before running off to do more important things?"

I have enough sense to glance over my shoulders before I speak my mind.

"Have I fucked you and left you dry in a past life? Or you one of those females that's always man-hating?" I snap.

"Excuse me?"

"Oh, now you want to act polite when all night long you've been serving your stank ass on a plate. All I'm trying to do is get to know you, form some kind of friendship since we have to work together," I whisper.

She narrows her gaze at me. Well, fuck you, too bitch.

"Why would you sign up for this show and you have no fucking clue what to do? Know what, never mind. Just understand that I will not lose because you're going to have to actually work," she spits.

My eyes roam her face as if she just lost her damn mind.

"What the fuck that's supposed to mean. No, I don't post pictures of myself eating, getting my nails done, or some borrowed quote while striking a pose every few minutes like you do, but that's because I am, you know....actually getting shit done," I fume.

"Our food is coming," she warns in a harsh whisper out of the side of her mouth.

I drain my glass while I let the waitress layout the third course of our meal. Tia reaches into her bag to produce a printed sheet of some kind during that time.

"Listen, let's just stick to the meeting," she suggests.

Not giving me the opportunity to speak, she goes on babbling. "Your home, the one you offered to do the filming in, can you tell me..., suddenly, she trails off. "Something you said before...how do you know what I do on social media?"

I say nothing as I chew my food. The silence stretches out while my knife melts through the steak while I cut another piece to put in my mouth.

"I asked you-"

"And you said we needed to stick to the meeting at hand," I remind her.

"No, I want to know," she presses.

"And dumb hoes are walking around here wondering why their men can't do right. They still don't have an answer and are living their lives, so..."

I place another piece of meat in my mouth.

"Luckily, I'm not one of them," she sasses.

"Yes, of course not," I reply, mockingly.

I narrow in on her hands, balling into fists.

"Tell me what your issues are with me."

If she was willing to hold back before, she's pissed enough to say it now.

"Okay, I'll tell you. I can't stand white boys like you that try to be black. All tattooed up, singing like you're all soul when you aren't. Trying to tell me there was no place for you in country or pop. Just like all these females getting the fake asses and lips, going to twerk classes...ya'll rape us of our culture to make millions."

My chewing slows to a standstill.

"Thank you for acting as a mirror, but I already know I'm not black. I'm this way because I'll admit, I'm a product of my environment. From the Bronx to the cell block, to being raised by a black woman because my own mother was too busy giving her ass away to any fool that would holler."

"Whew, now buddy, stories like that bit Vanilla Ice in the ass," she warns.

"I swear you are a rude bitch. How the fuck you come off trying to read me? God, I should have listened to Chana and Yosef, but I'm a sucker for big asses," I grumble.

"Oh, so that's what this is all about, huh?" she laughs. "I'm going to take this opportunity, but I would have never fucked with you," she chuckles.

I haven't had the urge to pimp slap a woman, but Tia might make the list.

"I've come to find the ones that protest the most seem to cum the hardest."

My comment takes some of the wind out of her sails.

"Baby boy, I hope you packed a lunch because you'll starve waiting on me to give you some play," she tosses back.

"Is that so? I don't think you even believe half the words you're saying right now, but I get it. You don't want to be another on my list. Put up a good fight, okay, but we both know I'll most definitely be dusting the cobwebs off your old coochie. That way, when your mouth is sucking my dick, and I'm stroking those walls, you can feel as if you tried," I smile.

Without warning, Tia rips the top sheet of paper from her tablet, crumbles it to throw it across the table at my face. My eyes register the cream-colored ball flying my way, but my brain is telling me that I must be dreaming. The connect is nothing but a light tap as the wad of paper bounces off my forehead.

Snatching up her purse, she pushes her chair back from the table.

"The ink has dried...and honestly, all of this is a dream come true. We have to work as a team, so I can only hope you can put on a good act like you've rope-a-doped millions of people already. I would say I'm flattered that you went through all of this in the hopes of getting with me, but the fact that you thought a little flash and money is all it would take for me to throw it back proves to me that I was right about you. The quicker you understand I'm out of your league, the better off you'll be."

I blink my eyes rapidly. I'm dumbfounded. I'm thunderstruck into silence. Wide-eyed, I turn completely in my seat to watch Tia walk through the dining area to disappear out of my sight. Even though she's gone, I know she's gone, I'm still glaring at the vacant doorway. Slowly, I straighten myself right. I come face to face with her empty chair. Reaching for the bottle, I refill my class.

I'll give Tia a point for one thing and one thing only. I did come here thinking that getting between her legs was going to be easy. Years of it being that way, just caused me to make an ass out of myself by assuming she would be no different from the others. Sipping on my wine, I replay all the shit that just went down. I'm making a mental list as I go, and at the end, I come to one conclusion. A wicked smile forms across my lips.

Tia Symone Jefferies just made her biggest mistake. She should have never told me I was out of her league. ME? I got pussy on speed dial. I'm selling out stadiums, breaking charts, and she thinks...Nah, baby. I don't know who she's fucked in the past or what fictional character her rude ass is holding out for, but it's going to be me she's going to be jonesing for. I can picture it now. The sex is going to be intense, rough, extra long, and sweaty. Jesus, my balls are so tight right now.

"Are you ready for dessert?"

I give the waitress a beaming grin. "Yes, I am."

TIA

Sliding into my car, I slam the door.

"Shit," I hiss as the shaking of the entire car reminds me that I need to handle this leased vehicle with care.

I hold my paper tablet in both hands to begin beating the stirring wheel. It does nothing to stem the frustration raging through me.

"Fuck! Fuck! Fuck!" I scream.

I should have known that all of this had a catch. Oh no, I couldn't have gained the spotlight due to my talent or my relentless hustle. It's the same damn thing, different day. I've been trying to make a name for myself for the last three years.

My entire inheritance was pumped into this company. Everything I have, my blood, sweat, and I'm still being locked out. These white people seem to be willing to pay top dollar to one of their own, but when I walk through the door, I'm shut out. Either the rich women clients regard me as if I'm an empty-headed, no talent designer, the straight male clients see me as a piece of ass, and the gay clients won't break ranks to hire a straight designer. Never does my actual knowledge and talent get taken seriously in this world of entitled ass snobs.

For once, I thought things had changed. Hell, it only takes one big job to change your future. This job was the fucking mother load, but nope this asshole is after what's between my legs and not what's between my ears. He didn't even realize he would have to be a part of the going ons. Clearly, I was dead on the money about him being a privilege asshole that made it rich off of every damn thing others have done.

"I won't...not...again," I huff while leaning over to grab the compartment car door open.

Digging in the area, papers, booklets, napkins all fly through the car till my hand touches what I'm hunting for. I growl at the HD image of the sexy ass tattooed man on the CD cover. The cheap plastic cracks in pain under the force of my fingers attempting to strangle the picture of Johnny Thicke's sexy ass in all his tattooed glory, wet from standing in the night rain. I curse myself for having this CD, five more at home, two vinyl records, and a number of his songs on a few playlists. Yeah, I'm a fucking fan. I got to admit, the man can sing. He looks fine as hell. I've been listening to his music off and on for a while in spite of the personal feelings I have about him. I'll take that information to my grave.

Cranking up my leased BMW i5, I reverse, switch to drive and speed out of the parking garage. Rounding the corner, I pause at the entrance for the arm to raise to allow me to exit. Leaning out the window, I toss the CD out the car. I hit the gas, and I pull the wheel, slightly left to swerve to ensure I roll over Johnny's face. Petty I know, but with no one to witness my actions, I have no shame giving into the childish urge.

CHAPTER FOUR
JOHNNY

"Take a breath. You'll be fine."

"Of course, I will be," Tia snips.

I bite my bottom lip to reframe from yelling at her. For the last two days, she's been a little bitch. Every time I tried to call her to discuss our first day of taping, she shot me down. I take a second to glance around before walking closer to her makeup station in the corner of the closed-off room in the restaurant.

"Your nervousness is going to show through," I warn.

Sliding out the chair to her feet, she glares at me. "The emotion is annoyance."

My strong hand closes around her arm to shake her into submission.

"Put away the resting bitch face for the moment," I growl into her ear. Another shake to rattle her brain and her legs are wobbly enough that I'm able to drag her around to face me.

"I heard the camera assistant over here talking to you, and that guy is full of shit. Look," I demand as I point across the room to the filming area. "Do not look into the camera. They are going to be panning in and out, which is going to take a second to get used to, but you will. Just remember, you're not doing porn. Those big ass mics are going to be hanging over head, just ignore. Act like everyone else is invisible and focus on the real people. I know that might not make sense, but you'll understand. And I'm sorry, but this is getting on my nerves," I admit. I pause to snatch a makeup sponge from the table to smooth out her nose. "You got somebody coming to hook you up?" When Tia looks confused, I sigh. "You know, um…beat your face, do your make up because the chick from the network is going to have you looking like a cakey goddamn ghost."

"Oh, yeah, yeah. The person is running late."

"Well, you don't have the pull to make the crew wait, so either the person is on time from now on or replace them. I'll stall for a few minutes," I offer after dabbing in the liquid makeup clumping under her eyes.

TIA

"Thank you."

I swallow hard as I steal a peek of the area. I thought I would be alright. For the last two days, I've practiced speaking loudly and talking slow and clear with Mother and Brit. Yet, here I am, when it's time to show my stuff, I'm ready to turn into a deer caught in high beams. I look at my reflection in the lit mirror. I cringe at what I see. I hate to admit it, but Johnny is so, so right. I look like a damn ashy zombie. Quickly, I snatch a wet wipe, clean my face, then grab my cell.

"Where the fuck are you?" I growl into my phone behind my hand.

"Look up, queen."

"Oh, thank God," I praise while hanging up. "We're running out of time."

"Chill, honey. My boy is a professional. It doesn't take him long to work his magic," promises Ryann.

The man tips my head back with a finger under my chin. "Praise the goddess you have good skin. Um, you gonna do something with her head?"

Ryann places a canvas bag on the stand. "I come to slay, bitch," he laughs.

The tension drains a bit. No longer am I alone in a sea of faces I don't know. No longer am I looking at myself as if I'm out of my element. Ryann pulls out, opens, and shakes out a custom wig with the baby hair plucked. Without a word, he switches to stand behind me while his friend, I guess I should get his name, blocks out the mirror to get to work. In no time, my hair is braided down.

"Are we going heavy or natural?"

I glance at Ryann for an answer to the guy's question.

"Make the foundation light, golden highlights...focus on her eyes, make them pop, but give her a bold lip," instructs Ryann.

The man tilts his head and nods in approval before leaning in.

"OMG, is that Johnny Thicke?" hisses the man.

"Shit, where? Where?" whispers Ryann. "Oh, my stars," he cries, clutching one of his $5,000 breast.

It wasn't till then while glaring at Ryann that I notice his amazing makeup and hair. Now I know why these two were late.

"Don't cause a person to slip with all the drooling ya'll a putting out," I huff.

The makeup guy cuts his eyes at Ryann. "I thought you said your boss is straight?"

"Chile, she is. She just being petty and pretending to be unfazed," replies Ryann with an eye roll.

"Oh," he mouths. "Sure thang, hunee," he mocks while dabbing the correct foundation for my skin tone into my skin. "Hoe, take my edges. Is that Jay-Roc," the man low shrieks.

"Who?" I wonder while turning in the chair.

"I thought you said it was just gonna be Johnny," hisses Ryann.

Righting myself in the chair, again, "I guess he and Chana came to watch," I shrug. "Um, my face," I press.

"Yeah, right," the man says in a mindless voice. He isn't even paying attention to me.

"Fuck, he's coming over here," whispers Ryann as he drops his eyes to the items lined on the table.

"Hoe, how do I look?" the man asks in a rush.

"Pimple faced, fat, and ashy," mumbles Ryann.

"Bitch, you-"

"Tia, hey!"

I smile at the light tap on my shoulder.

"Wow, you look good. Was I the only one to show up not production-ready?" I joke.

Chana is for sure on point.

"Well that's kinda standard. You never trust the network people to have someone staffed to see to your needs. I thought Johnny would have warned you about that."

I clamp my mouth shut. I won't tell her that I'm sure he tried to the many times he called, but I wasn't up to listening.

"We have a trailer behind the restaurant," she informs me.

"That explains it," I whisper to myself.

"Are these your clothes?" she asks.

I hadn't even noticed the garment bag laying across the nearby chair.

"Are those my clothes?" I repeat the question to Ryann.

"I pray to God it is," grumbles the makeup artist.

"Yes," remarks Ryann as he shoves his friend's shoulder. "Stop throwing shade and finish."

I take note of the change in Ryann's vibe. Gone was the joking to be replaced with a stiffness in his movements and lack of eye contact.

"You can use the trailer," offers Chana.

She outstretches her arm for Ryann to drape the bag over it.

"Done," declares the makeup man.

He steps to the side. I lean towards the mirror, blinking disbelievingly that the reflection I see is me. Flawless is the only word. He might talk shit, but he makes up for it in skill.

"You got the job, um…"

"Bianca."

"Alright, but next time you're late, that's it," I warn.

True to the custom of being extra, he jumps up and down, clapping like a fool. "No CPT got it."

I do a double-take at my reflection before walking away to follow Chana.

RYANN

I have to wonder why, when he hasn't gone on his merry little way. The fact that Bianca's thirsty ass is pawing on him isn't helping, either. Finally, I find an excuse to remove myself from the train wreck of Bianca looking like a fool. Instead of him staying with the person that clearly wants his attention, he follows me.

"Hey, hey," he calls out.

Damn him and his long legs. My two steps to his four were no match. He passes me to cut me off. Licking my candy red lips, I steel myself for a meeting that I wasn't in the right mind to have.

"Jay-Roc," I smile.

He locks his hands behind his back as if he has to hold himself back from causing a scene.

"You know that's not my name. Ryann, you look...amazing," he exhales as he takes me in from dark blonde wig to my Jimmy Choo shoes.

I have to remind myself to be kinda nice to him. Afterall, Tia and I are standing here because of him.

"Thank you. How is the rap game treating you? Still juggling it all?"

I said "kinda nice", remember. He catches my meaning.

"I'm still dropping hits, so yeah. Look, I'm sorry."

"Sorry, for...what? Keeping me a dirty secret for damn near two years? Or sorry for breaking up with me in a text when somebody saw us out? I'm confused," I mock.

Yosef works his jaw. I should feel a bit of pity for him. It took me years to come out and a few more to have the bravery to begin transitioning. Worrying about how you'll be accepted can be a bitch. I shouldn't be the one applying pressure when he's not ready. It doesn't matter that I look so much like a woman that the majority of the masses are fooled. If he's uncomfortable in the open out of fear of being discovered, that's him.

"I'm sorry for both and more. I, I," he stutters,

"No, I'm being a bitch. Your image is important. You're an established rapper. It's not like you're some one-hit-wonder that can afford coming out as being gay."

He sheepishly glances away as he sighs in thought. Fuck if he ain't the sexiest undercover brother I've seen. Buff in all the right places. Tattoos and a chiseled jaw that goes on for days. Just a tall dip of honey on a hot day. I sniff the air to inhale his scent. Gosh, I love the smell of a man. If I had lady bits, I know I would be wet. Instead, I hope that my tuck and tape job holds up under the pressure as my dick begins to fill with blood.

"So, are you here to watch?" I ask in hopes of breaking the sexual tension.

It doesn't help. Yosef hits me with those open, light brown eyes, and I'm falling.

"I'm going to be part of the team."

"Oh, really," I speak, slowly.

I'm gonna need more tape.

**

TIA

"How do I look?"

I pull back the curtain in the back of the single-wide trailer. Strolling down the hallway, I stop in front of the full-length mirror to take a look.

"Better than me," grumbles Chana as she gets up to stand behind me. "I looked washed up compared to you and Ryann," she complains while tugging at her dress. "Don't I?" she questions Richey.

I watch his gaze dart between my face reflected in the mirror and Chana's demanding stare. I can tell he's debating if he should answer such a personal question in front of me. He is supposed to be just the bodyguard.

"No comment," he answers as he heads for the door.

"He's scared to admit the truth. Where did you buy this?" She presses.

"It's not off the rack. Ryann's friends are making our clothes and the wigs are done by Ryann."

"No way!" she exclaims. She rubs the fabric of the pants suit that's hugging my hips to perfection. "The seam work is on point. I would have never known. That's good that you're using your platform this way. I'm going to have to pull Ryann to the side for a little chat," she says.

"So, what's the deal with you and Richey?"

I considered Chana pretending not to hear me, or to straight out tell me to stay in my lane. Yet, she doesn't even hesitate.

"I might as well tell you since you and Johnny are going to be..."

Be what?

"Richey and I are an item," she says instead of finishing the other sentence. "He's so loyal to Johnny that he wants to keep it a secret."

Leaving the mirror, I pluck a cold bottle of water from the cooler placed on the countertop.

"Why should Johnny care? Does it say in your contract as his manager; you can't date staff?" I wonder.

Chana chuckles. "No honey, I'm Johnny's sister."

A bit of water drizzles out my mouth at her reveal. "Sister," I repeat in awe.

For the first time, I pick up on the resemblance between the two. The height, the sun-kissed natural skin tone, the dark brown hair, the facial structure both Johnny and Chana shares.

"Yeah, he's my big brother," she confirms.

"So, he doesn't want the boss to know he's dating his sister," I smirk.

Of course, Johnny would have a problem with the help aspiring for greater. Fucking his sister was just too big of a stretch.

"Oh, he knows. My brother knows what's going on in his own house. No, it's Richey that has the problem. He doesn't want to disrespect Johnny by crossing the line," she tries to explain.

A deep crease wrinkles my forehead. "Huh?"

Chana rolls her eyes. "It's a silly code that Richey is hell-bent on following. See, they...meaning Richey, Johnny, and Yosef...well kinda him for his own reasons, all ran the streets along with five other guys that you'll shit yourself if I told you their names. Anyway, Johnny wasn't the oldest, but he seemed to be like the daddy of the gang, always watching out and stuff. So, when things got crazy, and the cops were knocking on doors, Johnny took the blame."

"R-really?" I say, slowly in a hush.

"Yeah. He toed the line," she nods with pride.

"B-but why he did that? Didn't he go to jail for a few years? Is that why?"

"He did it because he knew that the hammer would come down a lot softer on him because he was a poor white boy than his brown and black partners in crime."

"True dat, but jail," I stress.

"It wasn't easy for him, but Johnny was always smart. When he wasn't skipping school, he was making the honor roll. He was helpful around the neighborhood. All those facts helped the public defender paint a really good case in his favor of a white boy being led astray. Anyway, Richey promised to watch my back while Johnny was away. Then he started to watch my front, too," she winks. "To Richey, he owes Johnny his life. He doesn't want to mess that up."

"But why would you and him messing around fuck things up with him and Johnny?"

Chana's eyes widen as she drops her voice to barely a whisper. "Because I was only 17 and Richey was 20 when we started to...you know."

"O, Oh," I answer with a scrunch up expression.

Suddenly, we both jump when the front door to the trailer is jerked open. Johnny pokes his head in. Then slowly walks up the stairs to stand in the doorway. His narrow eyes land on the both of us. No doubt we look guilty, and he's trying to figure out of what.

"What's going on?" he questions.

"Nothing," Chana answers with a shake of her head.

Jesus, that look on her face is saying the complete opposite. Glancing back at Johnny with a smirk hanging from the corner of his mouth, I can't help thinking I was an ass. Funny how much 15 minutes gossiping can change things.

"Uh, huh," he moans. "I was calling you. Where the hell is your cell?" he complains.

Then again, maybe I wasn't completely wrong. Chana backtracks to the couch in the trailer. Feeling the creases between the cushions, she draws out the phone.

"Must have fallen," she smiles.

"You got to do better than that," he warns. "They've been waiting on you two to get started. You aren't here for girl talk," he replies.

"I said, sorry. Damn, John," she snarls while stumping across the trailer.

He steps to the side to let her out.

"I'm not giving you a personal invite," he snaps at me.

"I wasn't waiting for one."

I fall under his sharp eyes as he examines me while I get closer.

"Nice, very nice," he nods his approval.

"Thank you for your praise. Next time, I'll work harder to earn a pat on the head," I sass before I breeze past him out the door.

"No need to be butt sore. I tend not to do that kinda action on the first time out the gate…unless you get down like that."

I halt in my steps to look at him as if he bumped his head. With a chuckle, I shake my head to continue on.

"I don't give up," he shrugs. "Just keep that fire, and you'll do good, today."

I pause to let him open the door to the restaurant for me to enter first.

"So, you being an ass is all for my benefit?" I mock.

"If that is what will help you relax and not feel bad about your performance, I'm willing to be the bad guy," he mumbles.

Again, I steal a glimpse of him. "But you're not…a bad guy, huh?"

Johnny stops to examine me. "What did Chana tell you?"

I say nothing. I want the answer to my question. I hood my eyes at the sight of him raising his arms to run his hands through his hair. The flash of black and grey ink covering the canvas of his tan skin that bulges from the movement has my attention. His normal attire of a plain, blue t-shirt works to bring out the colors of his eyes, while his loose-fitting dark blue jeans that hang on his hips should make him blend into the background compared to what we are wearing. Yet, he's the type of man that can walk into a crowded room and without even trying will have all eyes on him. Johnny just oozes that 'it' factor that people are paying millions in hope of gaining. It's in his smile, his walk, in the bass of his voice, in the way he communicates with just a look…all so effortless it's scary. Even without the fame, he would still have been hard to ignore.

"We're ready," heaves Ruban. "Fuck, you've been scalped," he cries. "You gotta fix that, hurry," he demands.

"Shit," I hiss, touching my braids. "One, one sec," I call over my shoulder as I run towards Ryann and Yosef. "My hair."

"Oh, hun, come on."

In no time, my look is complete. In awe of my transformation, I only have a moment to make love to my reflection before I'm being ushered over to the tables.

"Turn," orders the woman for me to face her.

Being a pro at her job, she fits me with a tiny mic. "Testing, testing," she speaks into the hidden object while looking over to the side. A man with headphones gives her the thumbs up.

"So, why have the big ones over head?" I wonder.

"Because these catch all the whispers that those don't, so be mindful of the fact that someone is always watching and listening," she warns.

"Thank you," I smile.

"Alright, places. Guys, have a seat," says Ruban with a wave of his hand.

I stroll over to the table. The others all plop down, which left me the empty seat next to Johnny.

"Just focus on the important people," he whispers in my ear while making a circle of all of us at the table. "Let all of them fade into the background."

Licking my lips, I smile.

"You look fine as hell. You're sexy, too. Don't worry about that. This is just another meeting with your client," he remarks before pulling away.

Funny thing about reality TV is that it's the furthest thing from being real. Behind the scenes, the people are given cues, then left alone to improvise.

"Okay, so you all are meeting in the private area to introduce the members of the team to each other. Drinks will be brought in, and you will talk about the property, your vision, blah, blah, blah. Nothing too heavy, okay?"

"Yeah." "Okay." "Got it," rings out from the table in response to Ruban.

With nothing left to be said, it's go time.

CHAPTER FIVE
JOHNNY

Here I am coaching Tia when my mind is elsewhere.

"Lighting check."

Ruban gives me a few minutes to get over being so close to Tia. When I say she's looking like a snack, I mean that shit. I can't keep my eyes from dropping to her breasts to eye the deep cleavage in her pants outfit. Her slightest move rewards me with enough side boob to cause a distraction.

"Right, this is it. One...two...and action."

Well, damn. That's all we get. No lead-in, nothing.

"Thank you for coming in, guys," I start. "I think you all know me."

"Yeah, I think so," laughs Chana.

"I didn't mean to brag," I frown.

"No, of course not," my sister teases.

"Anyway, I'm kinda out of my depth here," I admit, sheepishly. "Standing behind a mic is easy, but this here is all new to me...and decorating," I trail off into a mumble. "Why couldn't you have signed me up for a cooking show?"

"Oh, you would have lost that one on the first round," jokes Yosef.

"Fuc-"

"Family show," interjects Tia.

I give Yosef a stare before going on. "Everyone, our ace in the hole, Tia Jefferies."

"Hi," she smiles. "This is my assistant, Ryann."

"My sister and manager, Channa, and I'm sure you know, Jay-Roc," I introduce. "This is the reason why Tia is here."

Leaning to my side, I produce a portfolio.

"I think you have what it takes to bring home the crown and earn me the title," I smile at her while laying the book on the table for Chana and Jay-Roc to take a peek.

I can see the surprise on Tia's face. If she had spoken to me before today, she would have been prepared, and I wouldn't have had to print shit off IG to make the book. No matter what, I'm going to make sure this show is the start of great things in her life.

"Well, we have competition, so I won't get too big-headed," she warns. "So, can you show me? Tell Ryann and I about your estate."

She's doing great not acknowledging all the equipment and lights around us.

"Yeah, Chana took pictures of the inside of the house." On cue, she presents them. "The place is over 10,400 square feet and built in the Pueblo Style."

"Wow, nice, oh, I like this room," remarks Tia as she passes the pictures to Ryann to examine. "I can do a lot with this," she promises.

"Well, what's your ideas for the first challenge?" I ask.

We were already given what it was to be. The scene of us getting the information, along with Tia and Ryann's brainstorming session will be edited into the show, later.

"Okay," Tia announces as she taps Ryann to bring out the drawings.

Out of the corner of my eye, I can see movement in the doorway to our private area. None of us glance up because we're so focused on Tia.

"Since the challenge is to showcase my strengths, I was thinking-"

"What the fuck is this shit?"

I still don't look up. If I had heat vision, the drawing Tia had created would be up in flames.

"I thought those were our drinks," whispers Ryann.

"Johnny, Johnny," grunts Chana.

"Who told him we were here?" I growl with my head down.

"Look, that's your homeboy, not mine," snarls Yosef.

"I guess I'll get my own chair, then," comes the voice.

Tia grips my arm, "Who is this?" she hisses.

"A constant hemorrhoid," I grumble.

Rubbing the bridge of my nose, me counting to five does nothing for my mounting temper. The cameras are rolling, and this is just the bullshit they want to catch on film. I can already mentally hear the awful music shows like this mix into scenes like this to add to the tension.

"I'm ready for my close up."

I lift my head, slowly to glare at Rafael. As if his loud mouth wasn't enough, he had to make sure he stood out even more. His 6 diamond chains, rings on every finger on his right hand, and with a bright, blinding yellow shirt that looked as if he was filling in for a deacon in a black church finishes his clown getup.

"I'll overlook the mistake of not including me at this meeting, but now that I'm here, we can really get started," declares Rafael.

He reaches across the table to grab the end of Tia's sheet. Her hand moves like quicksilver to plaster the paper down to the table.

"Who are you supposed to be?" She frowns.

Rafael returns her look with a scowl of his own. "I'm Johnny's right hand. You need to check your attitude," he warns.

With a tug, he snatches the paper away. His face transforms into an expression of disgust.

"What the hell is this? I know this isn't what you're bringing to the team because this ain't it at all. How the hell you even got in the door," he remarks, rudely. To stress his point, he crumbles the paper and tosses it onto the table.

The whole exchange takes only three minutes, but it seems like a lifetime. I open my mouth only for the voice speaking to sound like Tia.

"Motherfucker, if you don't-"

My hand shoots out to drag her back into her seat.

"You rat-faced, pus-"

"Ryann, sit down. Hold up," demands Yosef while he leans across the table to restrain Ryann from leaping at Rafael.

My chair falls back to bounce on the floor with the speed I get to my feet.

"You need to leave."

Finally, I get Rafael's attention.

"Did I hear you right? You telling me to leave?" he questions in disbelief, not moving a muscle.

"Get up, now," I fume while rounding the table to his side.

"I'll kick his fucking ass," promises Tia. "Who the fuck is he? Was this planned?"

"Gurl, you know every show need a Tamar Braxton," grumbles Ryann.

"I didn't sign on to be railroaded. I won't be played like this," shouts Tia.

Standing up, she begins to snatch at her mic.

"Sit your ass down," I growl.

"Oh, now you think to-"

"Sit your ass down," I command with an open palm to her chest. Snapping my head to Rafael, "Get the fuck up, fucker."

I don't let him decide. I march over, haul him to his feet, and drag him towards the entrance of the room.

"Hold up! So, you gonna treat me like this?"

I let him jerk his arm from my grasp.

"You need to go, okay."

I'm trying to control the volume of my voice while I'm still mic up. Dumb huh? I'm not thinking clearly at the moment. All I'm doing is trying to keep from smashing Rafael in the face.

"Wow, it's gonna be like that?" he tosses back.

"It's gonna be you choking on your teeth once I punch you in the face if you don't shut up and leave," I warn.

"But why they get to stay? Why Jay gets to be in all of this and not me?"

I grind my teeth. A fucking baby. A bratty ass kid is what he sounds like.

"He won't be on the show the whole time," I say.

"But he's getting camera time, and not me. That ain't fair. I'm your boy. I should be at that table….and that designer? I would have picked one better. You won't win with her," he spats.

"Listen, I'm trying to help you save face, man. Get the fuck gone, because I'm getting tired of telling you to step the fuck off."

I don't yell or even growl, but the way I'm glaring and the tension in my body lets him know I'm about to raise my fists.

"Fuck you. Fuck all ya'll!" he yells. "You wanna cut me out, alright, but just know...you fuckin' need me. That bitch in there don't know shit. When you come back to me, I'm charging you double."

I take a step in his direction, which causes him to stumble back, catch his footing, then make it for the main door. Taking a moment, I lower my head to rub my face. Never in a million years did I want shit to go down like this.

"That's not your fault."

I peek through my fingers to find Richey big self standing by me. Always on the job, he was no doubt lurking nearby to pull me off of Rafael if I couldn't stop kicking his ass.

"That was a string that should've been cut a long time ago," he goes on.

Pointing to the tiny mic, I roll my eyes.

"Hey, you tried to be nice," he shrugs.

"I know," I mumble. Shaking it off, "Where's our drinks?" I shout before going back to the room. "I'm sorry for that," I remark.

I'm greeted with chaos.

"Cut! Cut!" shouts the director.

Not following my orders, Tia leaps to her feet. "Get this off. I want this off."

Stage hands surround Tia in hopes of stopping her from destroying network property in her frenzy to remove the equipment. I stroll over to Yosef and Ruban.

"It was bad, huh?" I whisper.

"Yeah, but great footage," beams Ruban

"You set that up," accuses Yosef.

Ruban tosses up his hands. "How could I? Rafael doesn't even give me the time of day. The man's not in my contact list."

"No, I know it wasn't you," I ensure them both.

Ruban maneuvers to put his back to Tia and the others. "You got to get her back on board."

Without responding, I head for the storm.

"I warned you that there would be drama, and you said you would be fine," Chana reminds her.

"Yeah, within the competition. It's a contest, but who... what the fuck was that" points Tia.

"That was a so-call friend of mine. He has nothing to do with the show," I explain.

"Then why was he here?"

Invading her personal space, I grip her by the arm. "You need to calm the hell down," I snarl into her face.

All of this drama is getting to me. I get she was thrown for a loop, but she's doing way too much. Not caring about the eyes on us, I drag her into a side room. Slamming the door, I turn around to glare at her.

"Get your fuckin' shit together," I demand. "All he did was trash your designs. He didn't call your mama a hoe. Are you playing up to the cameras?" I wonder.

"What? No, no, I..."

She trails off. She takes a breath. "I thought you were setting me up. You and the network, that this is all a ploy to make me look like a clown."

Slowly, I press my back to the wall. I meet her searching gaze head-on.

"I am setting you up, Tia, but not for that reason. I don't like when people try to pull my strings, so I don't do it to others. Well, most of the times I don't, but this isn't one of them," I correct. "Listen, Rafael, the guy, we have a long history, and he can't see the writing on the wall. All you need to understand is this wasn't me. I'm not saying that the network won't play games for ratings. This here was a freebie, but it's something that I don't tend to continue to freely hand over to them. This," I twirl my finger in the air, "is all new to me, too. I've never done anything like this. Now," I say while pushing off the door to approach her. "I'm going to lay it out for you. I have millions. I'm not saying that to be a jerk, but to help you refocus. You need this. Are you going to let some knock-kneed motherfucker fuck up your chances?"

Tia inhales, then exhales. "No. No, I am not," she replies firmly.

"Good. Save all that anger for later when I start to get under your skin," I wink.

"Oh, I have no problems putting you in your place," she smirks when she comes to a stop in front of the door.

My hand hovers over the doorknob. I shouldn't have, but knowing we were alone in the room was all the excuse I needed. My free hand moves to rub her plump ass. "My favorite place is from behind. You can put me there anytime," I moan.

As quick as I made my move, I swing the door open to leave her to her reaction to my brazen come on. Tia hasn't seen nothing yet.

TIA

I'm motionless and stun. The only thing that's still acting as it should is the millions of butterflies in my stomach beating me to death, and the sharp tingling concentrated in my pussy. Suddenly, Ryann his at the doorway to stick his head in the room.

"What the hell are you doing?" I ask.

He takes another sniff of the air. "Trying to catch that fishy smell. He ain't get his fingers wet?"

I blink. "Boy, get the hell out of the way," I snap as I shove him to the side.

"Oh, come on, Boo. You wouldn't let him fuck you with those long, strong, tattooed fingers?" he finishes in a deep moan as he fakes a shiver.

My heated glare is both a warning and my answer.

"Go on and be the dumb bitch," he grumbles. Rolling his eyes, he shuts up.

"Are you able to continue?"

Smile in place, I nod my head at Ruban.

"Wonderful, um," he says louder. "The van is outside. We're heading to the property. The designs you were going to show at the table have been printed out. So, we'll make it so you will show your ideas for the room in the actual room, at the house instead of here, in the restaurant." He pauses to drop his voice to a whisper. "I'm really sorry about that, but in this kind of work, many people are rude, crazy, and cutthroat, but we...Chana, Yosef, Richey, Johnny we're not like that."

"Thank you," I smile.

Tapping him on the arm, Ruban gives me a beaming grin. He might look like an average guy in the midst of male runway hunks, but his inward glow gives him an odd sexiness that I'm sure many pretty girls tend to overlook.

**

The drive over to the house was a short one filled with cracking jokes. No matter how much I try to keep my professional mask on, I'm always pulled into the stupidness. I might only know Yosef and Ryann, but there is a weird ease that develops quickly between me and the rest. A man with a small handheld camera captures it all. Whenever I get lost in the weeds, Ruban offers to explain the reason behind the low jabs being thrown that makes everyone laugh.

Every now and then, I allow my gaze to wonder over to Johnny only to find him staring openly at me. I mean, he isn't even trying to hide it from the others or the camera.

"Wow," I breathe as I crane my head back to take in the massive home looming in front of me.

Taking a turn, I look out among the manicured grounds as the others step out of the van.

"That's what I'm saying, but stupid wants to sell it," grumbles Chana.

"I know I shouldn't say it, but the taxes on this house is way too much."

"Get rid of that ugly house an hour from here and bam," suggests Chana.

"How many houses do you have?" I ask.

"Four."

"Six," Chana corrects in a yell from inside the house.

"I know it's called reality TV, but you don't have to put it all out there, Chana," he teases.

Johnny places his lower hand on my back to encourage me to walk forward. Why am I dragging my feet? It can't be because I want to walk slow enough to not break the contact.

"Tia."

I turn to find Ruban at my other side.

"I want to show you the room," he says.

"Okay," I reply.

Not Johnny's hand but Ruban's now guides me into the house. My body doesn't respond with the same intense jolt. Instead of heat, I experience a soothing feeling that calms me.

JOHNNY

My gaze narrows on where Ruban's hand is resting on Tia. I don't give two shits that I was just doing the same fuckin' thing. The sight of seeing his pale arm covered in black hair makes it very hard not to become enraged. Normally, I would find it funny that he was trying to shoot his shot. Normally, if he managed to make a mark, I would shrug it off. In this town and tax bracket, there's always pussy in the sea. No need to have a falling out over trivial bullshit.

"It's the quiet ones," comments Yosef.

I stare at Ryann and Yosef daring them to say something else.

"Oh, chile," chuckles Ryann as he twists his ass up the steps.

"I'm just wondering how he's giving a tour of my home, that's all."

The lie stabs me in the throat coming up but passes smoothly through my gums.

"Hum," smirks Yosef.

Inside the house has been cleaned. Nothing but open space, I've never got around to decorating it.

"Welcome to one of my houses," I call out, teasing Chana. "I've made no major changes. Hopefully, you'll help me put a personal stamp on it to drive up the selling price," I explain.

"Actually, I plan to decorate it to the point that you fall in love with it. I'm telling you it will be hard to sell once you put some work in," she promises.

"Follow me this way," I instruct.

Just as I had thought. Ruban didn't know where the fuck he was heading before. Coming to the empty room with its cream-colored walls, large windows overlooking the side of the house, and gray carpet, I give Tia time to get her bearings.

"How do you feel about the flooring?" she questions.

"I'm willing to do whatever you want."

Shit, that came out a bit too deep, too sensual. Even she turns to raise an eyebrow at me.

"Happy to hear that. Luckily, I won't demand too much," she replies.

Is she flirting with me? I fight to keep my eyes on her face and not to let them drop to caress her visible breasts thanks to the low cut of her outfit.

"Um, are we talking about flooring, still?" asks Ryann with a raised hand.

I roll my eyes while closing the space between Tia and I. I can't stand Ruban hovering around her, but I can't show my ruthless hand so soon.

"What's your vision, Hun?" I ask in a soothing tone.

I take note of Ruban's arched eyebrow. That's right. Back the fuck up. You think I can't see what your cock-eyed ass is doing. Not only that, why the fuck he's even in front of the camera any damn way? He's the money man, not a part of my team or a fucking adviser. I swear none of these people here want to get a taste of the straight-up motherfucker I am deep inside. Nor is it a face I want the world to see. I refuse to be the no good, downright thug that I'm painted as.

For the next thirty minutes, we look over Tia's drawings to compare them to the actual space we're gathered in. I gotta say, she's talented.

"I know you have these here," I remark while waving the pictures. "But, now you're here, you got the vibe of the place, is there anything you would want to change to make it, you know...pop?" I wonder.

"Are you saying my idea isn't good?"

"Hold up, I'm not stepping on your toes. You're an artist, and you're sensitive about your shit. I'm just opening the door for change."

Tia crosses her arms while taking a turn around the room.

"Like what changes? You obviously want to say something?" she huffs.

I clear my throat. I can feel the pressure of the eyes and the lens on me. Jesus, I don't want to come off as a fool, but I want to connect with Tia.

"What if you made this an accent wall? Is that what it's called when you make a wall a bold color to pull the focus?"

"You got it, Boo," coos Ryann. "What color?"

"Well, the house is Spanish inspired, so...mustered yellow...or a deep red. I would change out the normal white crown molding trim and do a walnut or woodsy kinda thing to make it in place with the house. Maybe even switch out the crystal chandelier for an iron one," I shrug.

I won't look at Tia just in case her face is saying, 'Fool, stick to singing'.

"Hum. Hum," Tia moans.

Fuck I was off the mark. I'm getting ready to back paddle in hopes of saving face.

"I know I'm the assistant, but-"

"Those changes are really, really good," replies Tia, finishing Ryann's comments. "I never thought that your house would be Spanish themed. I did all of that planning off of what I thought you would live in...but you managed to surprise me," smirks Tia.

"Johnny, you can do the molding, flooring, and changing out the light fixtures," beams Chana.

"Hey, he made some good suggestions, no need to stretch his abilities," chuckles Tia.

"Shit, my boy was lead foreman for my Auntie when he lived with her in Canada. She made her money flipping houses. Johnny got skills outside of singing and producing," explains Yosef.

Ah, that's the look I was working for. That light of being more than what meets the eye I'm picking up in Tia's gaze.

"I'm not doing any flooring," I grumble as I try to downplay the whole interaction, "but I can get the other stuff down as long as the contractor does the rest."

"Cut!!" Shouts the director.

The older man is practically doing the two-step.

"Okay, okay," he chimes as he walks from behind the monitor that shows him everything the cameras are trained on. "Wait, wait," he says as he switches to a different single word while his hands flap in the air. "No bullshit, you really are trained as a contractor, carpenter, or whatever the label is?"

"Yeah, I've done it for what, six years while working on my music," I admit.

"Oh, my freakin' God," the man inhales. "The network is going to love this shit. Can you imagine, Johnny fuckin' Thicke…sweating, tattoos glistening, ass in the air bent overbuilding shit? The fuckin' ratings, man!" he exclaims.

"You opened your mouth. I hope you can deliver" smirks Tia.

"I can always deliver on what I promise," I smile with a wink.

The director is watching the two of us. Giving us his back, he whispers to the woman that's his shadow. I should watch it around these people. Slipping into your normal self is the danger of being on these kinda shows. You can't be on guard 24/7.

"I don't think having him working like that on the projects is a good thing," interjects Ruban.

"Why the hell not?" snaps the director.

"Well, the other celebrities might not get the same amount of TV time as he does. That might piss them off," answers Ruban.

"Then those camera hog assholes need to start watching fuckin' Youtube to learn a thing or two. Plus, they were going to have to get their manicured hands dirty any damn way, which is part of the show. He can't help that he knows what he's doing. You're the one that dropped that bag by not checking that box before signing him on for the season. No, we're going to use this for sure," says the director.

He's already fishing out his cell to report to the powers the be at the network while Ruban follows close in hopes of changing the man's mind.

"Oh hell, ya'll might get a show off of this…one of those remodeling ones," whispers Ryann.

"Tia wouldn't want a show with me," I tease. "I'm sorry. I'll be careful not to take too much of the attention," I promise.

She's not even listening to me. Instead she's rubbing her chin in thought as she watches the exchange going on with Ruban and the director. Suddenly she becomes animated.

"No, no, this is good....and Ryann, you might be right. I mean, I know you got your singing thing, but you can't deny we have a bit of chemistry sparking here," she comments. "I know how these things work. Yes, this is a good thing," Tia beams.

I tilt my head while Chana and Yosef look at each other after hearing what she just said.

"You're gonna use my feelings for you like that," I tease.

"Oh, feelings?" whispers Yosef.

"Yes, the ones that start below, then travel upward," Chana whispers back.

"Shit, I bet that down below is something else," Ryann joins in the whispering.

I toss the three a glare that sends them off to talk about Tia and I, behind our backs.

"But really, that's cold when you know I want you."

"It's called flirting, Johnny," she says with an eye roll.

"It's called me being dead serious about fucking you."

"You know I'm ten years older than you?" she tosses out.

"What you are is seasoned, not dried up," I correct. "I'll help you, though."

"In exchange for opening my legs," she scoffs.

"You're going to spread your thighs for me, no matter what, so I suggest you get all you can out of this," pausing I step closer. "Because I'm going to get every drop from your gushy pussy...every nut, every scream, and every prayer out of you, Tia...and then some."

CHAPTER SIX
TIA

"Mama! Mama!"

I freeze in the middle of the kitchen. I had hoped to have an hour to myself before Brit came storming my gates. I release a loud sigh, turn, and conjure up a smile on my face just in time for her and my Mom to enter the kitchen. Brit is wide-eyed with excitement while Mom is trying really hard to downplay her desire to hear about my day.

"So, tell me everything," demands Brittany as she jerks a bar stool out from the side of the island.

"Wow, so no love," I tease.

"Oh," she says, jumping to her feet. She scuttles over to me to place a wet kiss and a fake hug on me before going back to her seat. "Okay...so, how was it?"

"The first day of taping was-"

"No, not that. How was being with him...Johnny Thicke," she interjects.

"He's all she's been talking about," adds Mom with a side-eye.

"You didn't tell anyone at your school?"

"Come on, Mama," she sighs with an eye roll. "Of course, I did."

I bite my bottom lip to keep the stream of curses from erupting from my lips.

"Baby, I told you not to do that. It's not going to give you the outcome you're hoping for," I reply, slowly.

Brit drops her gaze. My heart plunges into my stomach. I know the reason behind why she went to school and told about the show. She saw it as her ticket into the 'It' crowd and a remedy for the constant bullying she's had to endure.

"They laughed and don't' believe me now, but once the show airs, that will all change," she shrugs.

I give Mom a slight shake of my head to stop her from talking. There is no need for her to go into her speeches about toughening up and not caring about what others say or think. At times, Mom really shows her age with being so out of touch with what my ninth grader is going through. It didn't matter that my nerdy daughter had a very small group of kids she talked comics, Manga, Anime, and K-Pop with. She just wanted to be accepted and the bullying to stop. In her mind, proving herself in the eyes of those bitches and hoes that ran the high school was the way.

Another day of hardship is what I know my baby has endured. Too black, too quiet, too smart, too thick around the middle is what she's told when all I see is beauty in her flawless skin. I see intelligence in her silence when she's weighing the words of others. I see whit in her when she comes back with a deep response. In her body, I see sexy curves that I'm sure actually pisses off those same bitchy girls because of the unwanted attention Brit gets from guys' heated gazes.

I've considered moving her to another school when this private one is draining my funds didn't seem to be working out, but the STEM program that Brittany has wanted to be a part of is only at this location. Of course, this isn't the only school that offers it. However, you're talking about her going to a different private school in a different county at double the tuition that I can barely pay now. I just don't know if her dreams are worth the damage. Although I know that these bumps in her youth are to prepare her for the gut punches that are sure to come in her adult life, I also know that kids aren't the same either. These girls are bitches, entitled little psychos, while the boys are rapist with high powered lawyers on speed dial.

Wanting to pick her spirits up, I spill the tea.

"Well, the day was awesome," I beam.

"I can believe that. Is this what Ryann dressed you in?" questions Mom with a critical eye.

"Yes, you like it?" I ask while giving them a full 360.

"Yes. No," The two say in unison.

"He made you look cheap. He's always doing too much to prove he's a woman. You're there for a contest, not to show all your assets," scoffs Mom.

"Ma is on TV, not some Youtube video. She needs to be at the top of her game. She can't hide she's pretty," remarks Brit.

"It doesn't need to be on display, either," presses Mom.

"I'm not here for the fighting, but Brittany is right. How would I look if I looked thrown away? I'm a reflection of the grade of my business," I explain.

"Oh, like that fancy car you can barely pay for or the office, and the staged photos you post? Your skills, talent is all you need."

I grind my teeth at Mom's comment. She can never just support me fully. She'll give praise, but then snatches it away a second later by pointing out a flaw.

"And did he make another advancement. Parading around like that, I think you want him to," frowns Ma as she examines me coldly from wig to painted toes.

"He? Him!" exclaims Brit. "*The* Johnny Thicke wants to get it on with my Mom? Oh man, you two will start dating and I'll-"

"Your Mom doesn't need a man,...and not one like him," interjects Mom.

"No disrespect, Grandma, but you feel every man isn't for Ma," sighs Brit.

"If no disrespect, you need to stay in a child's place," sneers Mom.

Silence creeps into the kitchen as Brit clams up. Bullying at school and at home. My baby is never rude. Nor do I want her to fear speaking her mind, respectfully. I love Mom, but like many times before, I second guess her presence in the house. All I did was open the door, asking for her help with Brittany's school and after school schedule. From there, she became a permanent fixture to the point that she rented out her house and moved in.

"I got to admit, Mr. Thicke really shocked me, today."

My shift of topic lights up Brittany's eyes.

"Really?" she sighs dreamingly.

"I got to say, I wasn't ready. I really should have taken his calls earlier this week to be ready. So, I was there...like a fish out of water with people telling me what to do, not understanding any of it, then he walks over to lead me through it all. It was like a fog lifting," I praise.

"Jesus Tia, you sure drunk the kool-aid."

I ignore Mom's grumble.

"Come to find out, he can do remodeling," I add.

"What, like changing a light? Or like you see on TV level?" asks Brit.

"From what I heard, today…TV level. He's going to be showing his skills on the first project," I answer.

"Hopefully those are all the skills he shows," grunts Mom.

Working my last nerve, I had to say something.

"Is this how it's going to be for the next two months? If you have an issue, keep it to yourself. This is an opportunity that I'm not passing up just because you're riding my back."

I thank God that He's chosen my words because I promise you, I didn't want to be this nice. I want to give my Mom the cussing out she has coming.

"I'm really proud of you, Ma. You never gave up, and here's your chance," grins Brit.

"Thank you…and we're a team, so it's *our* chance," I correct her.

I can see the look in my Mom's eyes. I've seen it before. I know what it stems from even if she will never admit it.

**

"I think we're going to win the challenge," I whisper, leaning close to Johnny.

From the stern expression on his face, I feel he doesn't share my confidence.

"Maybe," he response out of the corner of his mouth.

"Maybe? Are you watching the screen over there showing the recaps of what everyone was doing? Two teams didn't even finish, one designer clearly cheated by enlisting more help, the other celebrity was too busy looking good to help, and the last team…I don't even know what they tried to do, but it came out all wrong. We got this," I finish with a smile.

Turning my head back to the panel of judges ahead of us, excitement washes over me.

"All true, but one thing you didn't calculate."

I glance over and up to look into his face. "What I missed?"

"I fucked one of the judges, and the female hostess hates me because I didn't fuck her."

I must have blanked out while I try to understand what he just said.

"Did I hear you rig-"

"You heard me right," he snarls under his breath. "Fuck," he hisses. "I knew about Cindy being a hostess, but Sabrina on the panel is new to me."

I blink, slowly before looking forward, again. I couldn't pick up on anything, but then again, our footage hasn't rolled yet. The director was playing it smart by placing us last on the stage to ensure the viewers wouldn't change channels early.

"Next up...Team Tia and R&B singer, Johnny Thicke."

My feet won't move. It takes Johnny placing his hand on my lower back and guiding me to our marker. Is that a nasty smirk I see flashes for a second on Judge Sabrina's face? I didn't think nothing of the lustful glances from Hostess Cindy. All the women and gay men did that whenever Johnny was around.

The nervousness I had cast aside was back with a vengeance. I'm too busy trying to analyze every chuckle, every frown, every expression, and seeking a deeper meaning in the tone of voices and questions that I'm at too much of a loss to answer. Thankfully, Johnny is able to answer most of the questions. It takes him elbowing me to get me to respond. My saving grace is that I'm good at what I do, which means I know how to explain it in my sleep.

"Um, I really like your design, but I have to ask...why the wainscot on the ceiling?" inquires Chip, one of the judges.

"I wanted to pull off of Johnny's suggestions about giving the room an exposed beam look to make it more Spanish in style. Well, re-doing the entire framework is time-consuming and costly. With the wainscot, we laid it as planks, then ran beams going the opposite direction to create the look. Then with painting the right to left beams a light cream, and the spread-out planks going the length of the room a shade of walnut, it gave us the effect we wanted. In doing so, we were able to show people at home another use for the material to get a cost-effective outcome."

A nod of satisfaction is all I get from Chip.

"Alright contestants, if you will retreat to the waiting area, the judges will make their decision. Once they're done, one winner will be decided and one team...will be going home," replies Cindy.

We only make it to the hallway before I swing around on him.

"If we're booted off because of," I point to his dick, then drag my thumb across my throat to sign, 'You're Dead'.

He gives me that narrowed eyed stare I'm getting used to seeing whenever he's doing his best to contain his anger. We're not dumb. We both know we're still live with mics. I glide into the room, keeping away from the chatter. I'm not here to make friends. I might make enemies due to being standoffish but come on...none of these people are my friends. We've been taping for five days now. Talk has already started that me and Johnny were the Network favorites.

Sliding into the chair, I do my best to keep my feelings under wraps. He must know I'm on my way to getting in his ass because Johnny picks up a chair to carry it to sit in front of me. I remain silent while concentrating on holding on to the fake smile plastered on my face. I nod my head as he ticks off the list of why I have nothing to worry about. That might be the case if he literally didn't possibly fuck things up. Although I'm smiling, reflecting in the depths of my eyes is the threat I made.

"This is the longest thirty minutes," complains a contestant.

Man, that guy didn't tell a lie. Finally, we were called in, lined up, the lights came up and....

"Action!"

"This week, you were given the task to decorate one room that's your dream room. Although many of you rose to the challenge, a few of you proved you just wasn't up to the task," begins Carl, the male host.

"If your name is called, please step forward," Cindy hops in. "Team Johnny and Tia."

We step forward as ordered. Two other teams are called after us. I pray she hurries up. I'm about to pass out from holding my death in fear.

"You all are saved. Please return to the waiting room," Carl says with a smile.

I about stumble as relief washes over me. I glance back at the three teams still under the stage lights. One team will be named the winner and will be granted favors for the next challenge, one team will be at the bottom, while the other team will be booted off. John and I weren't standing there, but I'll take the pass onto the next task. Once back in the room, the production staff is ready to un-mic us and send us on our way till, tomorrow.

"See, told you," smirks Johnny.

"Why, because they have to keep the pretty boy on the show for as long as they can?"

"Well, yes," he pauses. "And because we were the best of show, but of course they can't let us win every challenge."

"I know how these shows work. I just don't want to be passed through based on who my partner is," I grumble as I fish my cell out of my crater of a purse.

Shit, for messages and six texts.

"And they aren't and won't," he promises while we walk towards the side exit of the studio.

He's going on about something, but I've tuned him out. With each text I read, my feet become harder to move until I finally stop.

Brit: Ma, grandma isn't answering her phone. I need to be picked up.

Brit: Mom, can you get grandma to come get me, PLEZ?

Brit: I can't stand that old woman. You know she sees me calling. So darn petty!!!

"Fucking cunt," I grumble under my breath.

That's what my Mom was, though; a bitchy, petty ass, nosey, dried up cunt. Now, this woman knows damn well what I'm doing. She knows I'm busting my ass off to make good on this opportunity, but since I didn't go along with her, last night, she's pulling this bullshit.

Now, what the hell am I gonna do? I left my car at Johnny's property this morning and road in the van to the studio. I would have to either, Uber or wait for the studio driver to get his slow ass in gear to take me to my car, which is in the opposite direction from the school. The fact that it's only a little after 11:00am means something has jumped off at her school.

Me: Sorry, I missed your messages. Phone was off for taping. Bump Mom! I'm coming. Are you ok, baby?

"You got me looking crazy talkin' to myself," accuses Johnny.

"Huh?" I ask with a start.

Damn, well I am just standing in the middle of the parking lot.

"What? Shit, that's no different than what you're used to," I reply. "I don't have the time. I need an Uber. I gotta-"

"What's wrong?"

"Brit needs to be picked up from..." I trail off to open my text to read her response.

Brit: In the office. They messed up my clothes, Ma. So, shamed.

My lips move while I read.

"I'm gonna beat those bitches ass. I'm so fuckin' tired of this bullshit!" I exclaim while I stalk off towards where I don't know.

"Hey, hey, what's wrong?"

"You got a car? Take me to Brit's school," I command instead of asking.

"Yeah, um, this way," he says as he points in the direction of a cluster of cars.

"This shit has to stop...and the school does jack shit," I continue.

I'm totally lost in the haze of my frustration. If he didn't stop at the passenger side of his car, I would have walked on. I'm still cursing a mile down the road. The GPS that he thought wise to use instead of me helping him navigate is the only other voice talking in the car.

"Is it that bad?" he questions at last as he pulls to a stop at a red light.

"Bad? Bad?! These hoes have no brains. They have been bullying her none stop. I don't know what happened between middle school and high, but I'm going to have to lawyer up because I'm going to grease up to kick some teenage ass."

"So, she knows these girls?"

"Two, no four of them, yeah. The rest are new faces. So, why all the hate?"

"It's over some young dick," scoffs Johnny as he puts the car in motion. "Dumb as fuck the shit these girls do, but I bet that's what it's all about. Is she smart, too?"

"Honor roll, excellent awards,...in gifted," I rattle off.

"And she got the boys trying to get in there, too? She's a threat to those girls. You know how it was in school. Has she had to throw any hands?" he asks.

"A little shoving, but she's always been able to run away," I answer.

"Not to tell you what to do, but, um...that might be the problem. I'm just saying, and telling you the code of the street, if you always running, there's always going to be someone giving chase. I promise you, if she bitch slapped one of those girls and put a hurtin' on her, they'll put some respect on her name, next time," he explains.

Turning in the seat, I give him my full attention. I don't know why I'm whispering, but I am when I speak.

"That's what I want to do so bad. I mean, I want to tell her to bust those girls up, but her record, and what if she loses?" I cringe

"So, what if she loses the fight. We don't want her too, but so what? It shows people that she isn't afraid to stand up for herself and she isn't going to take their shit. You can't win every fight. You know that going in, but it's the fact that you aren't scared that will make people think twice. But I can teach her how to kick ass. I promise she won't lose," he grins.

"Are you talking that windmill shit?" I tease. Talking to someone that isn't instructing to turn the other cheek, or to toughen up and take it is a blissful change.

"What? Shit, I would have been laughed off the block. Nah, I mean squaring the fuck up, busting lips, throwing elbows," he laughs.

"Oh, alright...I don't want my baby getting set up for failure," I chuckle.

The mood shifts. The tension vanishes.

"Are you going to tell me about Cindy and what's her face?" I wonder.

A deep frown settles on his handsome face. "Why the hell would I spend this alone time with you talking about yesterday news?"

"Well, I need to know if-"

"Listen, Tia, you don't have to be jealous of any other woman," he jokes.

"Asshole, I'm not jealous over some boney ass women. Since you like to share your dick like mints I need to know if any more will be popping up," I scoff.

Johnny tosses his head back in laughter. "A mint is a non-threatening candy, Tia. I promise you the size of my dick is very threatening, and the way I use it isn't for everybody."

Shit, don't look. Hoe, you better keep your thirsty ass eyes from dropping to his crotch. You hear me. Don't you fucking do it, the voice in my head screams.

It takes great will power not to sneak a peek in an attempt to measure him up in his jeans.

"Does that really work for you, this act?" I smirk as I wave my hand in the air.

He actually pretends to be thoughtful. He shrugs. "Never needed to go to these lengths before. Consider yourself my first worthy opponent."

"And your first loss," I add.

"It's still the first round. I haven't begun to fight," he teases.

"God help me," I pray.

"Honestly, I haven't weakened you...not even a tiny bit?" he inquires while placing a small space between his thumb and pointer finger.

"Right here, alone in the car, I'll tell you, so you better mark it down on your calendar." I inhale deeply, then let it out in a rush. I can't look at him, so I train my gaze on the speeding landscape outside his window. "You aren't the idiot I pegged you as. You shocked me that you can do all the things you did during the challenge. You don't seem to be too flashy like so many other guys in the game and," dropping my voice to a mumble, "you are good looking."

"So why not let me shoot my shot and let it hit?"

"Because it's you," I stress. "You might not get it, but you aren't the real estate man down the street or the doctor. You are high profile, and there is no way you can tell me you can keep us under wraps. How you think my daughter is going to take me fucking around with you, huh? Then when you're ready to move on, then what? No, thank you."

JOHNNY

My eyes scans Tia's side profile before I train them back on the road. I consider telling her that she's wrong. I know how to get pussy on the down low. My panty games aren't splashed all over the papers because I tend to mess with women that have something to lose. Women in politics, in high society, even a few that are married, some young and older, but all that would take our time together to the grave. I don't care that it's been rumored that I'm gay. I have nothing to prove.

For Tia to say I don't know how to set up hotel affairs, rent distant locations, and keep employees around that are paid damn good to stay silent, is crazy. Yet, I'm not going to confirm that I am doing just as she's claimed before. I'll just bask in the glory of knowing that she's starting to see me in a different light. That she's starting to see me as a sexual contender, too. Yeah, I know she only said I look good, but there's a lot in that statement. There is an attraction in that statement, and where there is attraction, there can become lust.

I turn my head to glance out my window to hide my wicked smile. I'm working this shit. Little by little, I'm digging a hole that in time, I'm gonna fill with my dick. Listen, call me an asshole all you want. I'm just not hiding what I want like so many others. Unless the dude is gay or deeply in love, trust me, there is a reason why he's talking to you about what happened on *Love and Hip Hop*. He ain't springing for Starbucks and lingering outside the office waiting for you because he's a 'nice guy'. Fuck no. He's hoping you'll take notice and give his slick ass a chance.

The rest of the forty-five-minute ride is filled with clowning on the other contestants from the show. I recognize the name of the preppy high school when I turn into the driveway. I call it a prep school, yet it's nothing but a charter school with fucked-up kids, wannabe thugs, and a wing for the brainy students. In a place like this, money from the parents ensures high grades to push their spoiled little darlings along, instead of actually teaching them that achievements in life ain't bought but earned. No wonder the school staff hasn't jacked up those girls fucking with Tia's daughter. No one on campus was going to speak against the purses and wallets that keep the lights on.

I lean back to give Tia room to stretch over to flash her school parent ID card to the security man standing in the air condition station at the gate. He squints his eyes at the piece of plastic, then does the same to Tia to size her up. When his gaze falls on me, his small eyes grow in acknowledgment.

"Hey, h, aren't you-"

"The gate," I gesture ahead. "Her daughter is sick."

"Y-ye-yes Sir. Sorry," he stutters.

I catch the second guard getting to his feet to have a quick glance into my car to see for himself what's got his friend all flustered. I smile and wave before zooming through the gate.

"You know they are radioing to the office," she sighs.

"I'm sorry," I mumble.

"Why?"

"Because knowing me isn't going to get your daughter the golden keys to the gate. It will for some that want to use her, and others are going to hate her even more. I'll be here," I say as I put the car into park in the round-a-bout at the glass doors.

Tia gives me a strange look before getting out. I quickly put the car in reverse and back it up a few yards away from the doors. I nod at her before she disappears into the stone structure that looks like the school should be in England somewhere instead of in the States. I'm fucking things up. I can see this getting complicated. Not with fucking Tia, but all the other moving parts that can become sticky. Yosef told me she had a daughter. He also told me that it was Tia's practice to not bring the guys that were busting out her back around her girl.

Friendzone, I think.

That's where I'm headed. I tap the leather wheel in thought. It isn't until I hear voices that I glance up. I don't know what I was expecting? I mean, Tia is a fine woman, so it makes sense for her daughter to be pretty, too. Then again, the girl is only half of Tia. Hell, I've seen two good looking people make some ugly ass babies, so it's the luck of the cards. I gotta say, luck shined. My eyes roam the girl. Her hair was in neat braids with weave adding to the length. Nice shape, clear dark skin, cute features that I can see some fuck boy trying to mess with her. Yeah, she's a stunner. That fact for some reason has me strangling the wheel while glancing around to see if there was an asshole trying to look at her.

What the fuck is wrong with me? It must be knowing that she's being bullied. On the sly, I switch off the AC in the car to crack the passenger side window.

"They did what?"

"They poured chocolate milk on me in the hall and started to mooo."

What, what the fuck is wrong with these kids?

"How did- what did the principal say?"

"He called them in like always, and like always, they made a lame excuse. The girl said someone pushed her and it happened. She gave a sappy, completely bogus apology and he took it."

"Fuck this! Bullshit, you hear me. I'm going to beat that bitc-"

"Ma," the girl begs, pulling on Tia's arm. "I just want to go home, okay? Where's the car at?"

"I'm getting tired of ignoring shit, writing letters, and coming to conferences just for these people to not care. I sacrifice a lot for you to go here," Tia cries in the direction of the front doors and office of the school.

"The car, Ma? Come on," begs the girl.

"It's not here," snaps Tia. "I caught a ride," she finally answers as she points to my ride idling.

Slowly, I close the window. Turning on the AC, I pretend to be playing with my phone.

"Wow, who brought you?" asks her daughter.

"Just, just get in the car," demands Tia with a shove.

Hurrying things up, I roll to stop in front of them. Tia slides in. Her daughter, well she doesn't move that fast after glimpsing me in the driver seat.

"If you get in, you can talk to him," coaxes Tia.

The entire time, the girl's mouth is hanging slack-jawed.

"Johnny," I say, offering my hand for her to shake.

"Mr. Thicke," corrects Tia.

"I don't know if I feel comfortable being called Mr. Thicke by a little girl," I frown before putting the car in motion.

"Mr. Johnny," suggests Tia.

"Johnny," I correct, glaring at the girl's reflection in the rearview mirror.

"I, I'm...who am I?" she asks Tia. "Oh, Brittany...or Brit, or hey you, whichever you prefer," she says in a rush.

"Never hey you, but I can work with the other two," I chuckle. "Breathe, okay. I'm a normal guy, believe me."

"Yeah, but famous," she gushes.

"Jesus," sighs Tia.

"I don't know why you're acting like that. I know you were nervous when you met me. You tried covering it up with that stank attitude, but I saw it," I tease.

"You were rude...to Johnny," remarks Brit in awe.

"No, not rude. She was stank," I repeat.

"I wasn't," snaps Tia. She has to turn around to face the backseat to drive home her point. "I was firm-"

"So was I," I whisper for only Tia to hear.

"I was setting the tone," she continues on, punching me in the arm. "I wasn't going to let you think that I was going to be a brainless push over like a few designers in the contest are."

"Oh, ma's not one to be walked over," praises Brit.

"Damn right," huffs Tia as she faces forward.

"So, are you on for another week or did you get cut?"

"I'm ashamed that you would ask that," I scowl in response to Brit's question.

"We're still in the running, but we didn't win," admits Tia.

"So what, you have another try to show up and show out. That's all that matters," smiles Brit.

"See, she gets it," I smirk with a nod.

I watch Brit from the back seat as she touches the leather of the seats in amazement.

"This is really nice. What kinda car is this?"

"A Maserati EV," I answer.

"Wow, so what other cars do you have?"

"This and one more," I reply.

"Really?!" They remark in unison.

"Yes," I frown.

"What's the second one? A Lambo?" scoffs Tia.

"You really think the worse of me, don't you," I tsk. "It's a classic 1971 Ford Bronco, black, no spinning rims before you ask...just a regular truck," I smile.

Yeah, shut you up, didn't I? That's right roll your eyes and snake your head around to look out the window.

I take note of Brit's shirt.

"Don't tell me you like Nautro?"

"You watch anime?"

"Of course, a young man such as Johnny watches cartoons," huffs Tia.

"Ma likes Bleach and One Piece, but I think Naurto is better."

"Baby, didn't you say you were sick?" grumbles Tia.

"Yeah," whispers Brit, dropping her head.

Brit tugs on the sleeves of her sweatshirt. She can barely contain her excitement. Honestly, I don't want her too. She such an innocent and sweet girl, which are both rare and dangerous.

"I can't take it being quiet. You can turn on the radio, Brit," I offer as I nod my head towards the buttons on the console.

"Okay," she beams.

Tia eyes her daughter when the girl leans into the front to mess with the satellite radio. She switches it on, listens for a second, then goes on to the next channel. Suddenly the smile on my face slips at the sight. I can't hide the shock that registers on my face. Brit is clueless, but Tia catches me staring.

"I like this song," she remarks as she places her hand on Brit's. "Leave it here. You need to sit back, baby before he gets a ticket."

I know it's her way of getting Brit to hide her arm from my gaze. I steal a glimpse of the girl as she sits back and begins to sing along to the Fugees, *Killing Me Softly*. A million questions flood my mind. None that I would dare ask with her here.

"Are you working on any new music?"

Her question pulls me back into the here and now, thankfully.

"Yeah, I am. I had to push back my studio time for the show, but I have something cooking and a few awards shows and specials to close out the year."

"We have all your records. Actually, Ma has the records. I just have you on my playlist."

I laugh at her honesty. She has no way of knowing she's throwing her mother under the bus.

"You look so much better in person than on the TV. Not that you look bad," Brit reassures me with a touch on my shoulder. "It's that, you know, some people need all that retouching, lights, and makeup to make them look good, not you though. We thought you looked so good at the Met Gala, didn't we, Ma?"

Tia shifts in her seat, refusing to comment.

"Thank you," I chuckle.

"Can I get a picture with you?"

"As soon as we get to the house, yes," I promise.

"House?"

Tia must be going through by the way she rubs her forehead. "I left my car at his house, one of his houses, the one we're working at," she changes her answer to clarify.

I bite my lip. Tia suddenly looks tired to me. I take mercy on her by taking control of the endless chatter on the way to the house.

CHAPTER SEVEN
TIA

What is this man doing? I should just give in, fuck him a few times so he can lose interest and move the hell on. All I wanted to do was the show. Now, he's becoming fast friends with Brittany. I know my baby isn't slow by no means. She completely understands that we're riding in this car all because of the show, and from what Mom dropped yesterday, because he thinks he has a chance. Even still, she's a teen that's going through and is hanging with a celebrity.

I'm like a caged animal by the time we reach the house. The car hasn't even come to a full stop before the door is open and my foot is planted on the cobblestone driveway. We are not friends. They are not friends. This isn't our life. Yes, I'm trusting that after the cameras stop, Brit and I will be better off, but we will never be at this level. Johnny isn't the cure-all to our mounting problems. He's just a means to an end, a hand to open the door. That's it.

I haven't been following the conversation thus far. My main focus is getting to my car and getting the hell out of dodge before Brit is drug further down the hole. I can tell he wants to pump me for answers that frankly are none of his damn business.

"Can I see what you've done?"

I go ramrod straight with my hand dangling over my car door latch. Why the hell she can't just shut up and get her ass in the car?

"You wanna go back to school?"

"No need to be nasty, damn Tia. Let the girl see your handy work. Come on," he whispers to Brit as he waves her up the steps to the front door. "You can wait in the car," he shouts over his shoulder before heading inside.

"That motherfucker," I groan with a stump of my foot. "I'm gonna, oh, Lord," I mumble as I cast my eyes towards the heavens.

I'LL BE GOOD TO YOU

I lean on the doorway to the first room we've tackled. Johnny, being the showman, he is, takes time to point out every detail and answer Brit's questions. I shift my weight on my feet while I listen to him give me all the credit when he and I know that he had a say in the design, too.

"Ma, you did an amazing job," praises Brit.

"What he didn't tell you was that he did some of the remodeling."

"I remember you saying that he was going to get his hands dirty," she smiles in his direction. "I really like the house."

"Hell, you've only seen a little bit. You can take a quick tour," he offers.

"Nope, I have to get her home, so-"

"When is the next time she's going to get a chance to look around," he hisses. "Go on. Oh, in one of the rooms is a mini-bar with sodas, snacks, and a PS4 with games and its' hooked up to Funimation Network."

I guess I have no power whenever he's around. Brit doesn't even pay me any attention as she speeds walk out of the room.

"This is Heaven. Take your time, Ma," she tosses back over her shoulder as she jogs away.

I know what he's setting me up for, and I'm not falling for it. I turn fast on Brittany's heels to play tour guide only for him to jerk me back by the arm.

"Why does she have those marks?"

Damn, jumping right in, huh?

"It's nothing we talk about outside of the family."

"I swear I'll shake your teeth loose if you don't tell me," he snarls. "Is she a cutter?"

I hold my hands up to tell him to lower his voice. "Yes," I hiss, "But not in a long time," I add.

Hands on his hips, Johnny turns to walk a few steps away from me as he curses.

"Is it because of those bitches at school? She fuckin' herself up over that?"

"The cutting phase was in middle school. The bullying started this year, her freshman year."

"Middle school? She was just a kid. How she even knew about doing that? W, where's her dad? Can't he help you?"

How did I get to this point with him? When did my life become the main topic of the day? We aren't friends. I should just drag Brit out of here. I don't have to answer him. So, why is my mouth moving while my mind is screaming for me to do the opposite? It's not like he cares about anything other than what's between my legs.

"I don't know who the father is?" I admit, shamefully.

His gaze rakes over me. In their depths is the assumption I knew he would have about me.

"Look, even the hoe of the neighborhood knows what a DNA test is, and you are a lot smarter."

Anger that I really shouldn't have towards Johnny bubbles to the surface. Maybe it's the fact that he thinks so lowly of me. Then again, why the fuck do I care? He's a kid compared to me. We're not on the same level.

"I was raped asshole."

A shock and pity mixture transforms his handsome features. My heated response steals his ability to speak.

"It happened at the end of my first semester in college. I was so careful at parties to make sure I didn't become one of, 'those' girls. Then it happens to me while I was walking back from the library. I told nobody for months. I guess I'm happy the fucker only left me with a bad case of crabs and a baby. I could have gotten aids."

I can tell he doesn't know what to say. Things are changing between us. I can feel it. His eyes are looking at me in a new way. He's thinking as he is processing. I'm betting his desire for me has just ran its course.

"Plan Parenthood on-campus help me. They got me connected with a counselor that helped me work through the emotional aftermath."

"You got balls for having the baby," he commits at last, after finding his voice.

"I thought about killing her, but...I don't know," I shrug. "I'm happy I didn't," I smile.

"How did your family take it? Were they okay with you keeping it?"

"Shit, I didn't tell my Mom. For her to throw in my face, she was right about me not going away to college? 'See, I told you. You thought you were so smart, better than everyone, but Life showed you that you are just like the rest of us.' That's what she said when I came back with Brit after I graduated."

All he does is nod his understanding. Casting his eyes above my head in the direction of the open archway, "Does she know?"

"It came out when my Mom and I were arguing."

"Just a slip of the tongue, huh? Yeah right," he grumbles.

My heart clinches. I blink rapidly over the concept that he might understand me.

"Have you seen a professional to help her?"

There it is again with a flutter in my stomach added. Why can't he just be an asshole? Fuck!

"We've done therapy, yes. Then we stop-"

"Your Mom had something to say about it?"

I don't answer. I just stare into his eyes.

"Tia, you need to do what's right for your baby," he suggests, softly.

"Which is what I've been doing by busting my ass with the show and doing what's right concerning you," I pause to hold up my hand to stop him from talking. "I'm hanging on by a thread, Johnny. I'm in debt. I got bills. I don't have the time to fuck around...and I can't afford to let Brit see you and me as more than what we are, which is nothing. Johnny, you are a dangerous fantasy. You aren't like the real estate guy in my building that I fucked around with. At least with him, there was a chance that we could have become more than bumping buddies. With you, I got no future. You're young, got money, and hoes to keep your balls from ever turning blue. You're still living your best life. Now, do you understand? Know what, I don't really care if you do or don't because it's just the way it's gonna be."

I'm not staying to listen to his response.

"Brit! Brit, baby...time to go!" I shout at the top of my lungs.

I bite my lip to keep from speaking. She wants to stay. I'm kinda thankful that Johnny doesn't try to use his pull to let her. Instead, he tells her he has things he needs to do, which could be a lie or not to get her to leave without too much drama. As he promised, he poses for a picture. What I don't expect is to be included. At the last moment, he reaches out to pull me close in front of him to face the camera. I should fight to put space between our bodies, but for once, I let it happen. I don't fight the warmth of his rock hard body. I sniff the air to inhale his scent of pure man, sandalwood, and evergreen. He wraps his arms around me. Cheek to cheek, I fight the urge to rub my face against the stubble of his chiseled chin.

"Say cheese."

Not a plastered smile, but a genuine one, I smile. Standing there in the yard of my dream home that would never be mine, Brit captures the moment in a flash of her cell.

Fantasies can come true.

The voice speaking in my mind causes me to break from Johnny. It had been years since I've heard the familiar, deep, calming voice of my grandfather. I'm rattled, and it shows.

"Thanks for the ride," I remark already at my car.

JOHNNY

For the rest of the day, I was in a foul mood. My time in the studio was a total waste yesterday. The beats I had created and sampled before I had been so excited to record to, were now lacking something that I couldn't figure out. The calls I received from artists in need of my personal touch have gone unanswered. After coming home, no bottle of vodka, whiskey, or beer could give me relief. No bowl of grade A weed could mellow me out. Sensing the truth, my staff and Chana stayed far away from me. Noticing that I was creating a dangerous mood in the house, I took it upon myself to stick to my rooms or to walks on the trails on my acreage.

I can't move on from meeting Brittany and what Tia told me. Shit! Fuck! To know all the shit they both have gone through has kept me from closing my eyes. Then the way Tia read me my rights before walking out pissed me the fuck off. How the hell she knows what I'm gonna do? I'm so goddamn tired of her telling me that I'm not good enough, that I can't be and do right by her. Yes, yes, I know that all I've said was that I wanted to fuck her, so I shouldn't blame her for her reaction, but she hasn't even given my ass a fuckin' chance. A fool can change his mind once he gets in deep to see that there's more, right?

The thing is...am I that fool? According to her, I'm nothing but a pipe dream that can't offer a woman nothing more than the eleven inches currently sleeping against my thigh. To be honest, now that I think about it, my ass has never really been in love other than one time in my life. The affair ended on a good note, but it was a relationship that changed my life forever.

"Damn," I growl as I jerk my shirt off the hanger.

The hanger can't stand up to the force and breaks to fall to the floor. Maybe I should leave Tia alone. If my pride wasn't so hurt by her words, I could admit she was right in her fears about me. Yet, those seconds I want them back. I'm talking about the seconds my heart stopped along with the world when I held her in my arms. Jesus, she felt so good...smelt so good, fit so fucking right next to me. Like I said, only once have I ever experienced that kind of heat and delirious excitement with a woman.

If I hadn't pulled her into my arms, I might have backed off after getting such a clear picture of all the shit and drama Tia has strapped to her back. I've given her the gift of a major come up with this show. It's now up to her to turn it into a dollar out of fifteen cents. Yet, I fucked myself touching her yesterday. I fucked myself meeting Brittany. I fucked myself by listening to the point that I feel for Tia to now see her as more than a cum bucket. That was the turning point.

"Johnny?"

I slow down enough for Chana to catch up.

"If it's not important, it can wait," I huff.

Making a sharp turn, I head down the hallway leading to the garage.

"It all depends on your view of important," she smirks.

Quickly, she shoves her cell in my face. My eyes widen, then narrow on the screen. Slowly, I pluck the phone from her hand. I swipe up to take in the media report. Without a word, I pass her the phone back.

"Care to release a statement?"

"When have I ever done that?"

"Are you saying that out of habit or because you don't want to?"

I glance down at Chana's phone one more time.

"I have some personal business to attend to."

"The press is going to be on you," warns Chana in hopes that I'll tell her what's been on my mind.

With a nod, I walk away. Now, I can finally stop hiding the smile tugging on the sides of my lips.

**

"M, M, Mr. Th-"

"I know you know who I am," I snap, cutting off the tomato face, sweaty, thin man that bruised his knee on his desk trying to reach me.

His fearful eyes fall upon the other staff members that have followed me into his office. I'm in full effect this morning. In a crisp Hugo Boss suit, I'm the picture of money and power. My tattoos on the parts on my skin that can be seen only adds to the dangerous vibe that I'm giving off.

"Come stand over here with the rest of your lazy ass staff," I order as I point my finger along the wall where the other men and women are lined up.

Backing up, I allow my angry eyes to settle on one person before moving to the next. Once I've made it down the lineup, I take the chair in front of the desk.

"You all know me, but it's this man's name you should be remembering. He's my lawyer," I gesture with my hand to the man standing behind me. "Mr. Cohen."

Shifting feet, side-eyes, and hard swallows are the staff's reactions.

Clearing his throat the leader of the pack speaks, "Nice to meet you...um, what brings you into-"

"You really have to ask that," I pause to read the shiny, gold plaque on his desk, "Larry. Don't tell me you all don't gossip in the teacher's lounge when you should be working," I reply, sarcastically. "I'll cut through the shit, okay. I want to know what is going to be done about the issues surrounding Brittany."

Thankfully, one of the teachers has the brains not to play dumb with me.

"Sir, we have taken many steps to handle her issues."

My glare causes the woman to step back, closer to the wall.

"What fucking measures? If that were the case, she wouldn't still be suffering every fucking day in your halls. All of you know damn well she isn't making up being bullied. Is it because she's black? Or is this school favoring the people responsible because they have money?" I sneer.

"W-what? Wait, Sir, I can promise you that-"

"I said I wanted to cut the shit, Larry," I warn. "She didn't toss milk on herself yesterday for shits and giggles. You called the girls in, but you didn't put a stop to what they are doing. Why?"

The man exchanges glances with the teachers in the room.

There'll be no help from them, asshole. If any head was going to roll, they were going to make sure it's going to be his.

"Well, the girls said sorry and explained it was an accident," answers Larry, weakly.

"So, every time was an accident," I mumble as I nod my head. "And those, the screens are hooked up to the cameras throughout the campus. Did you follow up to see if the girls were lying...or did you just take their words?"

Oh, I got you son of a bitch.

"Let me motivate you to get off your asses," I state ready to bring this to a close. With a crook of my finger, Cohen produces the paper I had him draw up. "I'll leave this here," I say, placing the stapled papers on Larry's desk. "Please explain," I order my attorney.

"Ms. Brittany is now under my services, thanks to Mr. Thicke. In the document, you will find a list of demands being requested on my client's behalf. Bullying is a serious offense that has led to suicides, mass shootings, and other preventable tragedies. We are sure that you wouldn't want to taint this school's reputation...nor would neither of you fine educators want civil suits brought against you due to lack of action."

See, that's why I like Cohen. He has a way of threatening a person in such a refine and sophisticated way.

"I'll say it a little louder for the people in the back," I remark, getting to my feet. "IF Brittany has any more drama and nothing is done to nip it in the bud, I'm going to use all my pull to fuck this school up. I don't care who those uppity little shits parents are, you better pump the brakes on what's been going on before I bring every goddamn thing crashing down."

Going to the door, I open it but stop short of leaving the room.

"Donuts are in the break room. Have a good day."

TIA

Well, last night was an eventful one full of me trying to keep Mom out of my business. I made sure to hit the mall to give Brit and I the opportunity to talk freely without ears listening around the corner or through the doors. Even still, she wanted to know what happened after I picked Brit up after she pretended to be busy. Fuck that shit. Brit felt the same way. Although, I'm sure she continued her prying on her drive to drop Brit off to school, today, but I know my baby was tight-lipped about it all. No doubt that will earn us a few days of Mom giving us her ass to kiss. Whatever.

Half of me wants to call off today's work, while the other half is secretly excited to be seeing Johnny later. I just pray he doesn't give me pity. I can't take being treated with kid gloves like I'm weak or something. I'm not. In spite of everything, I've done really well for myself. I'm determined. I'm strong.

I'm prepared for the shift, the change in our friendship. Yes, that's all that we've ever been, friends...and I use that word loosely. Co-worker is a better term. He's someone you see on a daily bases that you are civil too but can care less to know what's going on with them. Then once the day ends, you clock out to leave without a second thought of that person. I look at myself in the full-length mirror in my room. I recite all the warnings about Johnny. I remind myself that this is my big break. I tell myself that if there is a problem, the problem is with him, not me. I promise myself to stick to the plan and don't let personal longings get in the way. Shit, his dick isn't the only one. Turning to the side, I admire my profile. I'm still a knockout. Yes, I know I can get sex if the mood hits me.

Tossing the locs of my wig over my shoulder, I give my reflection a kiss. Hearing my cell ring, I already know who's calling.

"I'm on the way, Ryann."

"Gurl, the office can burn down for all I care. Have you been on IG this morning?"

With a frown, I open the app. After strolling the feed, I give up.

"Why? Who died?" I wonder as I turn off the light in my room to start walking down the hallway to get out of here.

"Shit," he hisses. "Are you friends with *The Shaderoom*?"

"Who?"

"*Balleralert?* Damn woman," he snaps.

"Calm down, I'll search for *Shaderoom*."

"Hurry up...*The*...then *Shaderoom* is all one word. You got it?"

"Yes, I have..."

"Hello! Hello! Don't tell me this girl just hung up on me. HELLO!!"

"That's me...and-"

"Yass, kitty!" he screams in my ear.

I'm too shell shocked to even notice.

"How is this...what they are saying isn't true," I insist.

"Baby, you keep telling yourself that, but a picture is a thousand words. Look at you...all glowing for the camera. Oh, and that look of lust in his eyes. How was it being held close to all that sex and man? Your fish got all wet and shit, didn't it?"

"Shut up," I snarl. "I told Brit not to post that picture," I complain.

"Wow, you trying to keep the good news from me, I see," he grumbles.

"There is nothing to keep," I hiss. "It's just a silly picture. He and I aren't together."

"Well, the World thinks so, and that's all that matters, hun."

"Fuck," I cry. "I have to disconnect my IG."

"Why?"

"You really think I want to be dragged."

"Dragged? Honey, these people are all for it. Read the comments. *'Oh, Johnny likes his women seasoned.' 'She fine ass fuck.' 'Shit, I'll tap that.' 'That's why he be coming up with all those lyrics.' 'I bet she be helping him hit those high notes.' 'Just proves he's one of us.'* He reads off.

"Seasoned?" I mumble.

"Tia, are stuck on stupid, or you just don't want to hear what I'm saying? You got a few haters, but overall, it's nothing but love. Shit, Johnny had already been picked up by us in the race draft. Now, he's just got a lifetime pass to all the cookouts. I say, let it play out. You don't have to come out the gate swinging to stump out a flicker that could become a flame if you'll get the hell out of the way. But I'll mind my own business. See you in a few."

He hangs up before I can even respond to his mouth full still ringing in my ear. One thing is for sure, I see the difference the second I walk out the door. Hell, how could I not when there are reporters camped out in the street before my brownstone condo. A stream of questions, shouts for me to stop to allow them to get a good picture causes me to act like a deer caught in headlights.

"Come on."

A hand arrests me by the arm to forcibly drag me down the stairs to the sidewalk. Out of normal reaction, I try but fail to get free.

"Stop."

This time, his face is close enough to mine for it to register who it is.

"Richey," I sigh in relief.

"Yeah, Johnny knew it was going to be like this."

"Hold up," I jerk back. "My car is over there," I say as I point down the lane.

Being the pro that he is, Richey keeps us moving while pushing back all the people that want to get a piece of me.

"We're taking this," he informs me.

Just as I was about to protest, the back door of the blackout limo opens and out steps Johnny. Instantly, the focus is off me as the reporters make a beeline to him. I marvel at the fact that he seems completely unfazed by the lens, mics, and the crush of bodies all fighting for a picture or a comment.

"Move back," he demands as he stretches out his hand for me.

A shove in the back from Richey gets me in arm's length for him to tug me towards the open door.

"I have my own car."

"Do you want one of these dip shits to cause you to flip your car all for a damn picture."

I close my mouth while the images of Princess Diana come to my mind. I want to refuse, but I want to live. Knowing he has won; he steps to the side for me to slip inside with him following.

"You need to do something about this-"

He places a finger in my face to signal for me to shut up. It's then that I notice the cell in his hand.

"I'm listening," he speaks into the receiver.

I have no clue what's being said, but it must be some heavy shit from the dark expression that settles on his face. I've gotten under Johnny's skin, but I never want to piss him off to this degree I'm seeing for the first time.

"Don't open the fucking door," he growls before he hangs up. "Go to the studio," is all he says.

I watch his side profile for a few minutes while I debate breaking the silence to complain. Then again, I'm not wanting a piece of the ass-kicking that he's barely containing. Nah, I'll just pick this battle for a better time.

CHAPTER EIGHT
JOHNNY

I clench my hand into a fist. I make sure it's the hand by the door to hide what I'm doing. Richey knows the signs. I want to punch, break bones, and this limo isn't moving fast enough to get me there. Son of a bitch! Then again, I consider as I tilt my head, this could be what I need. By the time we roll up, there is a crowd. Of course, there would be one. The motherfucker couldn't shit without having someone present to watch him wipe.

"Is it alright to talk?"

"Are you gonna be a bitch? Yes. Then no, don't talk," I reply in a rush.

The driver meets Tia's reflection in the rearview mirror to warn her to take my advice. All morning long, I've been imagining how it was going to be when I saw Tia since the picture of the three of us hit the internet, only for my excitement to be snatched by this bullshit. I glare through the tinted window at the scene, going on a few yards away. Waiting doesn't help me calm down. The raised voices serve to cause me to get even angrier.

Slowly, I shake out of my suit jacket. Next, I roll up my sleeves and loosen my tie. I open the door, get out, and all eyes are on me.

"Johnny!" a shout rings out. "All your asses are going to get the boot, now."

"Rafael, Whatcha doing here?" I ask. I slide my hands into my pants to keep from pimp slapping him.

"What you mean? I always come by the studio. Why you acting funny?"

I suck my bottom lip into my mouth.

"I told you a while back the studio isn't a hang out for your groupies. Are any of ya'll signed? Are you or you coming to record a track?" I question as I look the lazy fucks standing around Rafael in the eyes. "They aren't here to work. God knows you aren't here to work, so why the fuck you trying to get in?" I stress.

Rafael takes a step closer and drops his voice. "Why, why you making me look bad? You changed the codes on the door and told the girls not to let me in...what the fuck?"

"What the fuck is you're messing with my goddamn money," I growl, not whispering. "You post up with your fuck boys, and the artists don't want that shit. They pay damn good for the hour. This ain't a goddamn VIP at the club. You got a house. You need to stop coming and trying to take over my shit," I fume.

"Your shit!?" Rafael spats as he cranes his head back to examine me from head to toe. "When did this happen, huh!? When you started taking ownership!?"

"Nig," I exhale slowly as I force my fist to un-ball. "When was it never mine? What the hell have you brought to the table other than a bill? Get the fuck out of here," I order with a wave of my hand.

His broke down crew exchange looks as if they are trying to determine if I'm serious. My security knows I am. They move from their spot to start moving in.

"You don't want no smoke blowing, Johnny. You know I know people," threatens Rafael.

I swear his beat down is long coming. I mug the motherfucker in the face, which causes him to stumble back. Shock is clear on his face, then it switches to anger. I smirk. I want his froggy ass to leap. I wave one of the guards back. There won't be no trash talking later that if someone hadn't jumped in, he would have kicked my ass.

Oh yeah, he gotta throw hands now. I give him the first punch, but not another. I'm no worried. He and I have been here in the past. Nothing has changed to make the outcome different. My fists smash into his face with no mercy. In seconds, I have him on the asphalt. It's been years since I've gotten down like this, but the body knows.

"Johnny! Johnny! Is somebody going to stop this!?"

Tia's screams didn't stop my attack. The sound of a clip being pulled damn sure did. I freeze with my fist hovering over

Rafael's bruised and bloody face. A hand grabs him from under his arms to haul him from under me and onto his feet. Slowly, I straighten up. The sight is nothing new. I'm not even fazed at seeing guns pulled. Actually, it smacks of old times. Yet, there is visible fear on Rafael's face.

"So, this is how you rolling now?" I fume. "You playing in the wrong back yard, buddy. Sooner or later, these bulldogs are going to turn on you."

"Motherfucker, fuck you!" he yells.

No doubt having some metal backing him has made him brave. I watch his eyes pan to the side. Instantly, a deep, nasty frown twists his face.

"It's always about pussy," he spits. "I hope she fucks better than she looks. I'll just have to take a ride and see for myself."

In a flash, my hand snatches the gun from one of my men. Without hesitation, I level it at Rafael's forehead.

"You're trespassing," I snarl.

He narrows his eye on the barrel, glances at me, then they shift on last time towards Tia before he chuckles and backs away. I follow him and his weak army of wannabes pile into the car that I fucking bought for him to speed away.

"Move the studio to the warehouse and triple the security," I order as I hand the gun back over. "Let's go."

I'm in no mood for Tia to put up a fight. My fingers press into her arm as I grab her to speed walk her back to the limo.

"Next time something jumps off, you stay out of the goddamn way," I snap once I'm in the backseat next to her. "What the hell you getting out of the car for? We're you going to fight?"

"I'm not fighting a man, woman, or child over your ass....and there won't be a next time," she promises, hotly.

"None of that was my fault. You can't blame me for that shit."

"Toad the Wet Sprocket could be the blame for all I care. It doesn't matter. You can play at being a homeboy, thug, or whatever boys trying to be men games you want."

"You need to stop having a conversation with yourself about me when I'm not in the room," I suggest.

"Take me to my car," she demands. "If it isn't reality show related, I don't want nothing to do with it or you. Oh, and you need to Twitter, post, send up a goddamn smoke signal saying we aren't fucking or dating, too."

I pin her with an angry gaze that she's fighting really hard not to crumble under. Suddenly, I push the button to raise the soundproof partition.

"W-why you doing that?" she asks as she attempts to push my hand off the button.

"I'm doing it, so they don't have to hear me when I curse your silly ass out," I hiss. Leaning over into her face, "I'm sick of you thinking you know me. I'm tired of trying to prove to your cock-eyed ass I'm not the jit you say I am."

"You son of a bi-"

"I'll give you that assessment because you are so right about my old lady."

Tia blinks, not knowing what to say for a moment.

"You aren't going to the press?" she pants as her frustration elevates.

"I've never responded to anything they have said about me before," I shrug. "Something wrong with your eyes, because you looking at me like you wanna do something."

"You're a nasty asshole," she snarls.

I roll my eyes. "I'm also not making a statement because you're going to give me a shot. Oh, there goes the eyes, again. I have a doctor that can fix that."

"You've been smelling your own musk again, huh?"

No warning. No asking for permission or setting the stage. My hand captures Tia by the neck and jaw to give it a squeeze. I swear that's all I intended to do to release some of my frustration. So, why are my lips on her? Why am I pressing her back against the door while I lean into her body? Why am I fighting to part her lips with my tongue? Changing my tactic, I suck hard on her bottom lip. I smirk when her reaction is as I had hoped. She gasps from the pain of my roughness. Opening her mouth just enough, I recapture her mouth. This time, I won't be denied.

I slip passed her teeth to enter. Everything hits my sense at once. Her taste, the softness of her lips, the heat of her body, the rapid beat of her pulse under my fingertips, the feel of her tongue when she joins the fun of kissing me back. Shit! Tia is kissing me back. Jesus, the woman can kiss. The way she teases, how she uses just the tip to caress me, then retreats to allow me to deep throat her. Fuck, that sucking on my tongue is-

My eyes open, then roll back in my head when her hand seeks and grips my dick. Suddenly, space and air are coming between us. Neither one of us can speak. Wide-eyed, we stare at each other as we fight to regain our breath and wits. She attempts to push me off, but I tighten my grip on her neck. Wanting more, I go back in. If the treatment of my hand around her neck is rough, the way I'm making love to her mouth is the complete opposite.

"I'm going to get my shot, Tia."

I lean back enough to read her face and for her to see mine. A light flicker in her dark eyes then it's gone.

"We can fuck and get it over with."

Instead of giving in to the urge to strangle the bitch out of Tia, my hand loosens. I smirk. Licking my lips, I lean back to sit upright.

"Nah," I shake my head. "I change my mind. I think you misunderstand me," I say when I notice a flash of embarrassment creep into her expression. "I want more than a fuck. I want to fuck your mind...your heart. I'm going to own your soul, Tia, and the best part of it all is you're going to give it all to me. Know why? Because you've just shown me in the space of five minutes that you see me as a man...and not the boy you claim. A man, you'll find yourself trusting. A man, you'll find yourself falling for," pausing, I caress the side of her face with the back of my inked hand. "This time...."

I don't finish my sentence. Tia might have the qualities of another, but I'm to not blind to see she's so much more.

**

TIA

It's been a week since the kiss. For the last three days, I've been in the dog house with everyone. I fight to not let the pain of being outted of our group from showing when I enter the prep trailer for the late morning's taping. I shouldn't be pitying myself when I'm the one that did wrong, but I do. I had gotten to look forward to the laughter, the jokes, and the teasing that went on in our tiny group made up of Chana, Ryann, Yosef, and Richey whenever he wasn't trying not to cross the line not being on the clock. I had created a weird kind of work relationship with Johnny that he fought against every day. I wanted him to stop with the teasing. I figured out that he liked the press associating he and I as a couple, which pissed me off....and what led me to do what I did.

"Hi guys," I mumble.

I'm not surprised to only get head nods. With a sigh, I head over to the station Ryann has set up to do my hair and makeup. At least, he has to talk to me, but it's not the same warm way I'm used to.

"Hi, Ryann."

"Um."

That's all I get.

"Look, don't try to scalp me today, alright?" I grumble as I plop into the styling chair.

"Whatever," he whispers under his breath.

Jumping to my feet, I've had enough of this shit.

"Hey," I shout across the space to Chana and the others. "I'm sorry...really, really sorry, okay. I shouldn't have done that to Johnny."

"You think?" hisses Chana.

She's ready to kick my ass over her brother, which she should be. I hold on to the arm of the chair as she charges over to stand in front of me.

"He's been up your ass, running after you from day one, helped you get here, and you pull some shit like that on him," she snaps.

I cut my eyes in Ryann's direction to see if he's got my back. Of course, his ass doesn't.

"Listen, I said I was sorry. It was just a prank," I swear.

"You know what shit like that can do to a man's career," Yosef chimes in.

Frustrated, I roll my eyes and stump my foot. "All he had to do was say something; make a post, give a sound clip...anything to say he and I aren't dating."

"That's so fucking dumb, Tia. You walk around here like you don't like my brother when you know, we all know that you like it. You need to stop the act, girl, but no, you try to get back at him by hinting off that he's gay," shrieks Chana.

"Give some room," suggests Richey as he pulls Chana back out of my face.

"No, this hoe needs to know. I was rooting for you. I thought we were friends," she spits.

"I am your friend, Chana. I mean-"

"Nah, if he's beefing, I'm beefing, too," she snarls.

Wring her arm free, she marches out of the trailer. The three men stare at me.

"All jokes aside, what the hell were you thinking when you changed up the production of the challenge? My boy walked in to be blind sighted by what you did," remarks Yosef.

I plop back down in the chair. Chana didn't hit me with her fists, but I feel beaten up by her words. It only adds to the guilt of finding out what Johnny took upon himself to help Brittany. Hindsight is 20/20. Here I am always calling him immature then I go and prove that I'm the bratty bitch he says I am.

At first, whenever I thought back to the taping of three days ago, I couldn't stop myself from laughing. Johnny's reaction when the door to the location of a room in a warehouse swung open, and he saw the work I had done was priceless. The challenge was to design a room that revealed a secret about Johnny. After brainstorming, with Chana and Yosef, we agreed on decorating our space in trains and rats. Come to find out, Johnny's scared of both. However, I had other plans. The laugh they thought they would capture on camera of him walking into the room of horrors become a reaction of shock and barely contained anger. Not trains, but leather, wigs, fake asses, and sequins dresses. Not rats, but a huge stage to perform. Needless to say, the producers and director ate that shit up. Could it be that Johnny is living a hidden life? Could he be gay or even bi?

Funny how he claimed he never comments on what is thought or said about him, yet his ass was in spin mode in a hurry. I stood by to watch the side, one on one interviews the show does.

"What was that all about, Mr. Thickee?"

I was amazed at how he could hide his anger to be able to respond.

"The room is a reflection of how artiest in this industry have to hide you they are out of fear of not being accepted for their talent of their sexual orientation doesn't line up with what the public or fans think they should be. I know many, many artists, actors, and athletes that are hiding the people they are in love with and their truth out of fear or the shame of coming cleaning."

"But this challenge was to be a reflection of your personal fears," the person standing behind the cameraman reminds him.

"And that is a personal fear. I fear for my friends' stability. I fear for their way of life. I fear for their happiness because no one wants to be kept a secret. How can you say you love a person, but don't want to be seen with them? Even if the person says they understand, my friends still carry the guilt of being undercover. Trans people are losing their lives over this silly shit. So, yeah, it is a major fear for me. I wanted to use my platform to shed light on this issue and to give a nod to my friends that are struggling," he explained.

That challenge was our team's first win, which is another reason why I feel so low. Not to mention that what Johnny said was a slap in the face to me concerning Ryann and his struggles. His words brought tears to Ryann's eyes, who has had to deal with the threats and physical attacks.

I can't stay in the trailer another second. I have to make things right. Hell, I shouldn't have let things stew for this long. It took me a moment to track him down, but I was finally successful. I grind my teeth to see Chana standing next to Johnny, no doubt bitching me out.

"Um, can we talk?"

My world tips when he turns to tower over me with his cold blue-green eyes. I'm not ready to be this close to him. I know now that all I've done was to hurt and push him away in hopes he would give up his desire to make good on his promises of breaking me down.

"Not without me," grunts Chana.

"I'm here to apologies, Johnny. I was wrong for what I've done. It was childish, and you've done nothing but be honest and helpful to me. I own you so much...and you, too Chana. I betrayed you. I don't have friends, well other than Ryann. I really get excited coming here, seeing all ya'll. I hope that you can-"

Let's talk," interjects Johnny, cutting me off.

He doesn't wait for his sister to sign off, nor do I.

"I'm kinda hungry."

He pauses to stare at me.

"My treat," I offer as I point to a Chinese restaurant across the street.

"If I get the shits after eating here, it's your fault," he mumbles as he opens the door for me to walk in first.

I kinda low-key agree with him. The district we're filming in isn't that high class. While the other teams lucked up to get locations better than ours, the challenge of decorating a failing business to boost foot track landed us with a rundown children thrift store. If the smell didn't give cause not to spend your money, the crappy lighting and items thrown everywhere would do it.

"Drinks?"

Johnny frowns in thought as he eyes the sticky menu the older woman has handed us.

"Anything in bottle or can...not beer," I added quickly.

Not happy, he tosses the menu aside. Leaning back in the booth, he places his sexy tattooed hands on the table.

"I am really sorry about doing that to you."

"So, why did you do it?"

I take my time laying my menu down on the table as I chew my bottom lip. I debate lying. It would make it all so much easier, but I own him...so...

"I wanted to make you so upset that you would stop running after me," I admit.

"Ah," he sighs. "And maybe I would put something out saying you aren't an item."

"Well, that isn't a lie," I say, quickly.

He taps the table while he watches me.

"You're that scared that you'll lose your focus letting me in, that you would put that much energy into plotting against me. Damn, you really don't like me."

"No." The word comes out a bit too loud. I glance around the empty restaurant. "No, it's not that I don't like you. It's just," pausing I shake my head. "You really expect me to believe that you want to rock with me? Of all the women you could pick from, you want me and my ten years older, in debt, with a ninth-grade daughter...and my past," I say in a whisper.

"Tia, we all have a past. Shit, I spent a few years in jail, after selling dope, beating guys up in the streets, stealing cars, growing up below the property line, with a Ma that was the project's hoe. Not that I want to compare dick sizes here, but I think I got you beat on the fucked up past."

I drop my gaze.

"And as for the age, you wanted to park your ass on that spot. I came in, knowing you were older. Don't look it, but I never cared about it. In all truth, that turned me on since my biggest love was an older woman."

His revelation was like a bomb exploding between us. I open my mouth to speak, only for the woman to pick this time to return with our can Cokes.

"Are you re-"

"No, we're not ready," I reply in a rush. "Yes, we'll call you when we are," I finish with a wave of my hand. Leaned up on the table, my eyes wide, I press him to go on.

"I'm taking you into my circle of trust with this," he warns.

"I promise, Johnny."

He leans up, too. "So, after I got out, Yosef's Ma got me from around all that legal shit. She knew I went down for everyone, and I guess it was her way of paying me back. I went to live with her sister, Yosef's aunt in Canada."

"She the one you worked in construction for because she flipped houses," I add.

"Right...and she's the one I started fucking around with, too...when her husband wasn't around."

There goes my ability to keep my mouth closes as it hands agape in shock.

"Oh my God," I whisper. "I think I might have seen her. Yeah, she came to visit them once. Is she on the short side, thin, kinda soft speaking, dark with curly hair?"

Johnny nods with a smirk.

I cover my mouth with my hand, but my muffled, "No," can still be heard.

"I was in love with that woman," he admits.

"So, ya'll under one roof. Her husband never figured it out?" I ask, amazed.

"Honestly, I think he knew, but I think they had an open marriage. He had his side piece, and her's lived in the house. They didn't have any kids, so it was all consenting adults. I never disrespected him."

I can't believe it. I can't also stop seeing Johnny in a new light either. I mean, the man is getting ass left and right. Yet, knowing that he's had an affair with an older woman that I'm aware of is an eye-opener for me.

"How long did it go on?"

"For years. We started up five months after I moved in. I still flow back even after I came back to the States and was making a name for myself in the industry."

Now, that right there doesn't sit too well with me. Is he still hooking up with this old bird? Hell, why am I getting in my feelings? It's his dick, right?

"You two still-"

"No, I was getting too crazy over her, and I knew it. I needed to break it off. We both knew it was time."

I search his body language for any hint of lingering longing for the woman. I can't find any.

"If you wouldn't have shut me down, I might have told you that age to me isn't a number. Twenty- two to forty...maybe forty-three depending on the woman is my limit."

Another bomb. Damn, he just keeps on dropping them on me.

"So, you've dated older than me?"

He chuckles. "Yes, Tia, I have. There's a level of calmness that comes with an older woman. Not to say that I haven't fucked up and gotten with some insane, older ones, but overall the older women come with wisdom, confidence, without a desire to always have to be in the streets to be seen, and they love to fuck. Perfect," he smiles.

His gaze moves slowly over me as if he's trying to see if I'll fit in that category of, perfect.

It is perfect, Tia. He just described you.

I shake the voice off in my mind. I lick my lips.

Damn! Don't do that. Shit, he probably thinks I'm flirting. Wait, am I flirting? Do I want to flirt? Yes, yes I do!

I'm driving myself crazy.

"How is Brit doing?"

I blink. It takes me a second to understand what he asked.

"Good, really good. She said everything seemed to change for her one day. She's giving credit to the picture we took, but I know it's not that."

Johnny's face remains expressionless. Reaching over the table, I touch his hands. His eyes drop to take in my dark brown hand on his tanned, inked ones.

"One of her teachers let slip what you did. She actually told me to thank you because those girls needed to be put in their place."

"I didn't want your baby to start hurting herself due to being bullied."

What did he just say? I wonder.

His thumb caressing the back of my hand is wreaking havoc on my pussy. I stick with a safe response.

"Thank you."

He chuckles, lifting his eyes to look at me.

"I got a confession to make. I'm the one that leaked your address to the reporters."

I smirk. "You create the problem to be the hero of the day."

"Kinda," he laughs. "I did it because I like being connected to you. I was hoping you would have gotten used to the idea, too."

"Shit, no wonder you have so many number one hits. You got a way with using words to tie a person up," I huff.

"Fuck, I wanna tie you up; on your knees, or with you on your back, ankles attached to the sides of the bed, spread wide to take all my length," he whispers.

"I don't need my insides re-adjusted."

How the hell did we get on this topic?

"I know I'm a big dick motherfucker. That's why I'll take my time getting you ready," he says, pausing to flick his tongue at me. "My spit mixed with your cum will make it really easy to stretch your pussy, and it will feel good when I feed inch by inch into your tight hole."

I freeze in shock. I know I didn't just-

"Yes Tia, you just moaned, and it won't be the last."

Suddenly, I remember something important.

"All this verbal fucking is nice, but I don't want any trouble." When he looks confused, "With your homeboy."

I attempt to remove my hand; however, Johnny's not having it.

"Rafael is a nasty, two-faced, I think racist, which is funny when he's always acting black, grudging holding son of a bitch that's been in my pockets and living in my limelight from the day I met him at the Synagogue in Canada."

"You're Jewish?"

"Yeah, Chana and me. Richey is a straight-up Italian Catholic. After Yosef mended fences with his Dad, he took after his white side and dedicated himself to the faith."

I nod. We're getting off track though.

"Well, Rafael thinks I'm the one that broke up your bromance."

"I bet, but he knows he's full of shit. I've been trying to cut that cord for a long, long time. Anyway, he's not stupid, either. I'll let him talk shit. He can say I'm the one that's pussy whipped, and I switched out to save face in front of those fuckers he's trying to impress. I don't care," he shrugs.

I tilt my head. I must have lost my mind with my pride because what I say next is totally showing the hoe I hide inside.

"I guess what you're saying is I can't use him as an excuse for not giving you a piece."

Suddenly, Johnny's eyes darken. It's a sight that I want to make happen more and more. The fact that I'm the cause of it makes me horny ass hell.

"I think I wanna be one of those 'perfect' women on your list."

Johnny inhales, slowly as he hides his eyes under hooded lids.

"Nah Tia, you won't make the list."

Is he turning me down after I'm finally-

He continues, "You're on a list all your own, sweetheart. In fact, I know it's a mistake doing this, but I want it...you so goddamn bad," he admits, hotly.

Neither one of us needs to read the text messages chiming on our cells. It's time to get to taping. Digging in my pocket, I toss a five-dollar bill on the table. He does the same to add a fifty-dollar bill to the table. I stand to my feet with him slipping out the booth to tower over me. I give into the urge I've been fighting for weeks. I roll up on my toes to touch my mouth to his. This time, I'm not holding back. I give him a glimpse of the little freak I can be. Sucking on his tongue, nibbling his bottom lip, I let him take over the kiss, but not the experiences. My hand moves between our bodies to grab his dick.

"I can't believe this is all you," I breathed into his mouth. "I need a private viewing."

"Is that so," he smiles as he pulls me closer by my hips.

"Um," I moan. "You might have to take your time fucking me, but I'm going to suck all of this," I say, tightening my hold to let him know what I mean.

"Jesus, Tia. I'm gonna choke the shit out of you."

"You can try, but I'm a deepthroater, baby…gagging only makes me wetter."

Johnny's eyebrow arches. "Are you wet now?"

Shifting my stance, I open my leg. I don't have to say a word. He lowers his mouth along with his hand to maneuver under my skirt. My lacey panties are covered with the evidence of my arousal. All he had to do was touch the front of the material. He didn't have to go lower and slide his finger under the side to touch the juices on my waxed pussy lips, but I'm happy that he did. He takes his time coating my clit with the moisture before he penetrates me up to his knuckle.

"I don't know who you were fucking with, but you are too damn tight, Tia. I'm going to enjoy breaking your back and poppin' this pussy. Pussy like yours is going to be gushy, messy. The kind that will talk back as I dick it down and beat your walls. Ah, that's it. I can feel you clenching around my fingers. Lord, your muscles are strong. Yes, you're going to be a problem for me."

Suddenly, he fills me with his entire finger, then he adds another, then another.

"They're watching us, the restaurant staff. Should I stop, Tia?"

I don't speak. Instead, I force his hand deeper as I sway my hips to draw him deeper. He chuckles, followed by a moan.

"I'm going to fuck you after the taping."

Yes, I said that. Just like I'm riding his fingers in the middle of this restaurant without a care. I'm a closet freak, which only those men I mess with have the joy of learning. I don't know what Johnny was expecting, but he might be getting a lot more than what he thought.

Slowly, he removes his fingers. Looking me in the eyes, he begins to lick my wetness from his digits. Holding his wrist, I begin to lick his fingers, too. Not fighting him, Johnny feeds me all three. I open wide to take and suck them in a slow, sensual way as he follows my movements with his narrowed gaze.

The sound of the metal bells hanging from the restaurant door to signal a customer is in the building gets our attention. I slide my tongue between his two fingers, nibble on the tip of one, to finish with ingesting a finger whole before backing away, completely. Johnny steps close to kiss me roughly. I love it, giving it back to him.

"Um, you're both are needed back on set."

Even still, we share a heated promise before we listen to the assistant that was sent to bring us back.

"Thank you," Johnny shouts to the cluster of staff that were lingering around the corner as we walk out.

CHAPTER NINE
JOHNNY

I'm floating on pure fumes as we go back to the set to tape. I don't want to be here. By Tia's heavy glazed over eyes, her mind is miles away with mine fuckin' the early morning and afternoon away. My lack of interest is going to show when this episode airs on TV. I know the entire crew knows by now why. Call me creepy or downright nasty, I don't care, but I lift my fingers to my nose to take a smell of Tia's dried pussy juice.

SHIT, I hiss mentally as I readjust my growing dick.

"So, after this, you have to-"

"Cancel."

Chana narrows her gaze at me. I can see her head moving to take in the sight of what has my attention.

"Well, I can move the meeting back for an hour."

Giving Chana my full attention, I shake my head as a devilish grin appears. I'm a giddy motherfucker.

"Cancel," I repeat, stressing my meaning.

"Oh, OOOO...cancel, as in all day," she smirks.

"Now, we're on the same page," I nod as I go back to undressing Tia with my eyes.

"You'll never make it to the house," Chana states. "I'll book you a room," she chuckles, "But make sure she can walk so her daughter won't know," she adds.

"Yeah, kinda like what you and Richey do when you fuck on the go?" I tease.

Chana opens her mouth to deny it. "I can smell cunt and nut sweat, Sis. You need to carry wet wipes," I laugh.

"I'm not confirming anything...but I'll pick some up, today," she mumbles as she types on her cell.

Getting up, I put my plan into motion. You actually think I'm going to hand over another second to bullshit when I can be deep stroking in the tightest pussy I've had in a long time? I take my time to stop, smile, and talk along the way towards my two targets. The chief cameraman and the sound guy. Once I'm over in their little circle, I get down to business.

"Hey, um, listen, I have other plans for my day," I pause to glance over my shoulder at Tia to let them understand me, clearly. "I'll pay you 3 grand to break some important shit," I offer.

Tom and Jerry both look at each other as if I'm crazy.

"You're willing to pay us-"

"Yes, yes," I ramble. "You need to keep those earphones off more often, man."

Suddenly, Jerry, that's not his name, gets bold.

"3 grand, EACH," he remarks.

"EACH," I and Tom, not his real name, repeat.

"Yeah, if he wants to go play that bad, he'll pay," Jerry grins, confidently.

I chew the inside of my jaw. Why the fuck people just can't do you a solid, nowadays?

"You have Paypal or Cashapp?" I growl.

"Are you fucking really gonna-"

"Shut up and let the man pay us," interjects Jerry's bottle thick, eyeglass wearing ass.

"Whatever you do better work. Even if you accept the payment, I promise, I'll get my money back," I warn as I accept the men's pay.me links.

I walk away, head down as I go through the motions of transferring not 3 grand, but 6 GRAND out of one of my accounts. I swear Tia is the most expensive romp I've ever had. The loud sound of things crashing and falling down causes my head to jerk up. I watch in silence at the quick thinking of the two men. They might look dumb, but the fact that they made sure to cast the blame of the broken equipment of a few low-level workers proves they were smart.

"You just couldn't wait, could you?"

My gaze doesn't break from the drama going on across the room as I answer Yosef.

"I don't know what you're talking about."

"See, that's why you never got a part in a movie. You can act worth shit."

I laugh while I backhand him in the chest.

"Everybody go home!"

My face drops into a deep frown. I make a show of snapping my fingers and kicking an invisible can in mock anger.

"Can you give me a ride?"

My pupils dilate at the throaty sound of Tia's voice. The way her eyes dropped to stare at my crotch when she said, ride, makes me smile. Yosef doesn't point out that she came to the set in her own car. With a sweep of my hand, I let her go before me for the door. Once outside, it's a race to my car. Chana must have seen us because her text with the hotel info chimes my cell.

"The hotel is 10.7 miles away."

"Good, just enough time to play."

I have to focus on backing out the car at the feel of Tia's hand on my dick.

"Jesus, your dick is gonna feel so damn good," she moans.

I steal a glimpse of her zipping down my jeans. Without hesitation, she removes my granite dick.

"No underwear," she says with a lick of her lips. My wish is granted when her head drops, her mouth unhinges, and she ingests my dick in one passing. My eyes widen as she keeps on going downward.

"Holy fuck," I groan as my head falls back to land on the leather headrest.

Cars zoom by while mine is at a standstill in the middle of the fucking road. I've lost all ability to do two things at once. Her lips touch my pubic hair. Her throat clinches, and the most heavenly sound of her gagging fills the car. With a rush of intake of air, she comes back up. That look on her face; eyes red from straining, mouth gaping wide. I hold my breath at the sight of Tia producing a long strain of spit attached to her bottom lip, dangles in the air until it bathes the tip of my dick.

"I got myself a freak," I groan.

"You got nothing if you don't fucking drive," she winks while she spreads the moisture down my dick to give her hand enough slick to jack me off a few times.

Slowly, the car is put into motion. I try once again to focus on the road, to navigate through the goddamn traffic, only for my attempts to go up in flames.

"Is this what you want, Johnny?"

I do a double-take when I look over at Tia.

No longer is she sitting correctly in the passenger seat. Instead, she's leaning on the door, dress up, legs wide, and minus the panties I had to push to the side in the restaurant. My eyes burn the hairless, plump, dark brown pussy lips. For once, I'm happy this car is an automatic. Reaching across the space, I caress her pussy.

"You know I want to be here," I whisper.

Taking my wrist, she watches my expression as she penetrates her body with my fingers. With a bit of force, I fuck her hard. With each withdrawal, the glistening essence of her body coats my fingers.

"How do you want to be fucked?"

It takes her a second to get her mouth to do more than moan in pleasure.

"I want it hard...make me scream."

Finally, the god awful traffic comes in handy. Switching to the side of the road out of traffic, I quickly put the car into park and turn on the hazard lights. I waste no time.

"I need a taste," I announce. "Get that pussy over here."

I don't know if she heard my order. What I do know is that she feels my mouth when I maneuver over the gear shift to drop a kiss on her hairless lips. That's all it takes. Tia opens wider; her right leg rests on my headrest, the left on the dashboard. I relish the feel of her hand on the back of my head. Her hands entangle in my hair to force me deeper. I'm drowning in the sweetness of her creamy nectar. The tip of my tongue tastes her from her clit to the end of her opening. Like a dog, I repeat the action.

"Eat me, please," she begs as she uses the muscles in her legs to move her ass up from the leather seat in hopes of catching my tongue to fuck her.

Instead, I lock eyes with her as I figure eight her clit. Tilting my head, I suck and pull on her pussy lip before I start beating the hell out of her clit. Needing more space, wanting to see the pretty pink inside I've been dreaming about, I shove her leg up and back to her chest.

"So fuckin pretty," I whisper while I lower my face to give her what she craves.

We both groan at the contact when I stab her pussy with my tongue. My two fingers pull back her lips to expose her swollen clit. Slowing down, I softly simulate kissing, deep throating her pussy before latching on to her entire pussy to hum and suck.

"Fuck! Get your mouth open. Shit!" she yells while she tries to climb up the car door.

I don't let up till her legs are shaking, and I see her eyes roll back in her head. Quickly, I attack her parted lips to give her a taste of heaven. My fingers fill her again to pump her pussy in time with the movement of my mouth on hers. Her eyes are closed while mines are open. I don't want to miss a twist of her face. I tease her by rubbing the callous of my thumb across her clit.

"I need to get you somewhere," I say more to myself than to her.

Breaking into traffic, I'm a crazy man on a mission. Forget the hotel room. I make a left at the next light. I've passed an overgrown, vacant lot the last two days on the way to the offices we've been decorating for the reality show. My car might not be built for the off-road driving, but it manages to roll over the uneven ground and brush as I wheel the vehicle through the covering until we are well enough hidden from the road.

Car off, I reach over to jerk Tia out of her seat and into my lap. A second later, I change my mind. She might as well be a goddamn rag doll by the way I shove her out of the car to stand in the New York bright sun. She's as ready as I am. Open palms on the hood of the vehicle, her ass thrown back, she glances over her shoulder. I can barely lift the hem of her dress, release my throbbing dick from my pants, lift an ass cheek, and rub the mushroom tip of my dick at her wet entrance before she's demanding for me to enter.

The pressure of her pushing back in hopes of forcing me inward is mindboggling. The squeeze only verifies what I already knew.

"Sweetheart, I can't afford to split your cunt, if I want to get more of you later," I say as I pull my dick back.

My hand bites into her waist to make her cease her efforts.

"Oh shit," she groans, dropping her head to the car.

Inch by inch, I give her more, thrust a few times, pull back, then feed her more when I press inward. My legs are getting a workout from the strain I'm putting on them, but I've never been a one-sided lover. I lied when I said Tia was tight. This woman is a vice around my dick. Of course, I'm sure my size has a lot to do with it, combined with the joy of knowing she isn't run through.

"I can take it, Johnny...fuck me," she begs.

Testing the waters, I pick up the speed, giving her more of my length as I go. Sure enough, all I hear are moans and curses of pleasure falling from her lips. I widen my stance, and with the use of my hands holding her hips, I thrust forward while pulling her back till I'm all the way seated. Filling her completely causes a gush of juices that bathes my nuts. Knowing there has to be more, I rotate my hips to make the seal even tighter between us.

Playtime is over. Quickly, I slide my arm under her right thigh as I turn her to the side to lean on the car as my other arm snakes around her waist to hold her. In this position, I can glance down to watch my white cock disappear in her chocolate hole. With no barrier keeping me from going deep, I begin to fuck the hell out of Tia. My rough hand yanks down her dress top to give me access to her breasts. Through her bra, I squeeze her nipple, and her pussy goes wild around me.

One of her hands grips the hood of the car while the other is holding her belly. I shift my hips, and I know for a fact she's feeling my dick in her stomach. With each stroke, she's keeping my dick wet with her cum. It's like she's leaking. Her pussy is taking a beating. I don't let up as I lean into every move in my attempt to tattoo my name on her pink walls. So hot, so tight, so sticky wet, her pussy is the Grade-A shit. I'm losing it. I was warned. Ain't it a bitch that I find the right combination of good pussy, a woman that can suck the meat off a chicken leg, smarts, beauty, and it's a woman that I can't play like a fiddle to the tune of my fame and dollar signs. What I can do though, is fuck her so well, I turn her ass out. Sexing Tia is just the last shackle clinking shut to tie me to this woman.

I'm sweating like a raging bull. I know my face must be red under my natural tan. My hair is limp. I don't care. I'm not stopping. I reach back to jerk my shirt over my head in hopes of cooling myself off. That shit doesn't work.

"Come here," I pant.

Pulling out, I step back. Tia's foot drops back to the earth, and she wobbles on her feet.

"Come on," I order while I drag her to the trunk of the car. "Face down," I say as I expose her ass.

When she tries to defy me, I chuckle. Using her hair as a rope, I pull her head back as I penetrate her with one thrust.

"I changed my mind, I'm going to destroy this pussy after all," I growl in her ear.

"Yes, fuck me, ...oh, that feels so good. Ugh, my side," she yelps.

"If you relax, it will get better," I promise. "That's it, sweetheart. See, you can take it," I praise. "Do you ever go dry?"

Thank God the car can take the shaking and the weight of our bodies, too. The heat only makes things wetter, stickier, and aids the slip of my dick's entry. The slapping of our bodies connecting hard and in rapid timing echoes through the clearing. Placing my foot on the bumper, I gain a new level of penetration to the point I swear I'm ramming through her cervix. Even still, Tia keeps crying out, begging for more of my length. I don't know if she's crazy. Honestly, I don't care. I'm nowhere near being done with this cunt.

Falling back, I tilt her world when I lift her to sit on the trunk. Getting down on my knees, I taste and clean up all the residue my dick has created. With more room, I can open her legs wide by pushing them back to give me access to her pussy. She might have thought I was dirty in the car. Now, I'm fuckin' filthy. My thumb circles her asshole to use the spit from my mouth to moisten her hole. Without warning, I plug her ass up to the knuckle of my thumb while I stab her soft pussy. The gasp and moan that trembles from Tia's lips is all the encouragement I need. Her hand on the back of my head and her riding my face is a sure sign, too that I picked the right one.

"Let me drink your cum," I say before I latch onto her pussy to massage with my sucking mouth.

"You wanna drink it, huh? That's it...God! Eat me...I love you in my ass, Johnny...Oh, I...I."

Whatever she said after that is lost in translation. The same gush that has been coating my dick rushes into my mouth as her body begins to shake. I take my time to lick every inch before I stand with my throbbing dick in my hand.

"I wanted to cum around your dick," she whines as I pull her closer to the edge of the trunk.

"Oh, you will...again," I smirk.

This time, I enter her slow and damn near faint from the action. I watch in awe as Tia exposes her breasts to squeeze her hard nipples. Dipping my head, I open wide to suckle.

"You like being fucked and sucked, huh," I chuckle at the feel of her pussy quaking around me.

"Cum in my mouth."

Her request causes me to look up from her chest. Surely, I heard her wrong, yet I can't stop staring at her lips.

"I want you to cum down my throat."

Okay, I did hear her, right. For sure, my dick surges to let me know that he heard her, too.

"You need to shut up," I snarl as I straighten up to fuck her hard with my diamond chip dick.

"Please, Joh-"

My hand around her neck is to serve to shut her up. Instead, it makes matters worse. Tia's eyes narrow, mouth open...looking like the wild, willing woman that she is makes my nuts tighten to the point that I see spots.

My inner clock tells me we've been at it for over 45 minutes. My cock and balls are begging for me to let loose, while the greedy bastard in me is telling me to not stop till Tia's pink turns red. Yet, she won't shut the fuck up. Every moan, her filthy mouth, her pleading is messing with my head. I'm over here

CHRISINE GRAY

counting sheep in hopes of adding a few extra minutes to the party.

"Fuck," I cry while pulling out.

Sure, fuckin way, Tia manages to drop to the dirt before me. Still not sure, I grip my dick in a chokehold until she takes control. Our eyes lock, she lifts up while drawing my dick into her mouth and down her tight throat. Seeing her strain to fit all of me...the heat, that goddamn gagging is enough to end my fight. I seize her head between my hands as I fuck her mouth once, twice. The pressure of cum leaving my body makes me stumble forward. My grip on the trunk keeps me from falling. I'm in a flabbergasted daze while I watch Tia suck me off till the last drop of creamy, thick cum is ingested.

**

"Have dinner with me."

I can tell that my request throws her for a bit. Rolling over to settle myself between her legs, once again, I nuzzle her neck. Yes, we actually made it to the hotel. From the moment we crossed the threshold we've been at it. I can tell she's amazed at my stamina. I know Tia's rocked my fucking world with her never go dry pussy, her bottomless throat action, and the shit she's willing to do to get off.

"I told you that I knew feeling you, tasting you, hearing you moan, and move on my dick was going to be a problem for me," I pause to look into her eyes. "I need to know if that's going to be an issue?"

I search her face for an answer. I'm opening myself to this woman after just a few weeks of knowing her. A few would say I'm crazy...that the pussy must have messed with my mind. Those few are fucking fools because I've been catching feelings for Tia the second she shut me down during our first meeting. That rejection and the one in my house pissed me off, but it made me want to be better to prove to her that I can make her happy. Isn't that what being in a relationship should make you want to do; be better, do better, want more?

"Here or..."

"Out, Tia," I answer, slowly in hopes she understands what my answer means.

Even if she doesn't understand the weight of what I'm proposing, the rest of the world will. To date, I have never been photographed or attached to anyone in public.

"I've worked hard not to bring men around Brit."

"I'm not *any* man, Tia. *I'm the man*...and I'm not talking about who am but what I want to be to you and Tia whenever you're ready to let me," I clarify.

I see the flash of fear in the depths of her eyes. The fact that this is what she wanted, to have a man that would love her is a deep desire of hers and to finally having it laid at her feet is scary as hell. As for me, I have no fear. I know what I bring to the table. I know how to love a woman, cherish her, and make her the center of my universe. Have I done it a lot in the course of my life? Nope. That don't mean I don't know what to do.

"We'll take baby steps, okay. All you have to do is be willing," I say.

"Oh, I'm more than willing," she moans as she reaches behind my ass to touch my nut sack.

I brush my lips against hers. "I'm not talking about that, though. Are you willing to give this a chance?" I question, seriously

I feel more than see her smile.

"Yes," she replies on an exhale of breath.

TIA

I said, yes. I wasn't agreeing to marry Johnny, I know, but it feels just as important. I want to consider calling Ryann to yell it in his ear. Yet, I want to hold onto the secret for a little longer. Then again, his smart mouth ass wouldn't even be as excited as I am over the news. He and everyone saw us when we came back to the set after our restaurant foreplay. I'm sure the assistant that found us blabbed to everyone with ears the location of his finger, which were in my mouth at the time. Nah, all Ryann would want to know was how was the dick, and I'm not going to tell him about all of that.

Who am I fooling? Of course, I'm going to tell him. Sex this good can't be kept. Jesus, it was damn good. I always wondered why older women went for the younger catch. Although, every man isn't created equal, but goddamn if Johnny just snatches every experience of dick out of my entire mind. The sheer size was enough to have me fighting to not run away. Then when he started to use it, shit I was close to forgetting my damn name. I know I curled his toes a few times, too but I didn't think to the extent to warrant going out in the public. I mean, a selfie is one thing. Walking hand in hand is another.

Coming out of the shower, I hear the voice downstairs. I mumble a curse under my breath. I was so hoping to be gone before my Mom came home from wherever she's been in her failed attempt to punish Brit and I with her absent presence. I sit at my vanity, lotion up, then sit to look at my reflection. Tilting my head to the side, I focus on the new custom wig Ryann gave me, today. It's not as blond as the one tucked in my closet. I actually like the honey brown highlights throughout the black, wet waves of the silky locs. The asymmetrical cut that stops a few inches below my right ear is a work of art.

"Pride comes before a fall."

My gaze shifts to the person standing by my bed.

"It's not pride, Mom. I'm just trying to decide my makeup," I sigh.

I watch her take in the two-piece Greek style, satin dress that ties high on my hip and the high heels. She shakes her head as if she's pitying my dumbass. Since I don't ask for her opinion, she gives it. No shock there.

"Still biting off more than you can chew. I'm gonna enjoy watching you fall on your ass with this one."

I don't speak. Instead, I go on with doing my make- up.

"You actually think you're better than a younger woman that he can get. The man is rich, Tia. You have nothing in common with him, but you like to get fucked, and he doesn't mind fuckin' you up and over." She laughs. "You're a joke," she chuckles.

I hope she can't see me strangling my makeup brush. I refuse to let her know she's getting to me.

I shrug. "Well, I'll be ready for you to tell me how I couldn't keep him satisfied when it all comes crumbling down," I smile while I get to my feet.

"Yes, I well. I guess Brit is old enough to finally know her Mom isn't the saint, but is a mediocre slut," she sneers.

"You know, I hate that you have to watch me pimp myself out. So, why don't you leave."

She freezes. A weak laugh trickles through her twisted smile.

"Oh, I see. All of this show and attention really has you thinking you're all that, huh?"

"No," I remark as I shimmy into the skirt. "I'm just sick and tired of putting up with your shit. Why are you still here? I have no more money. I mean, that is what you were hanging on for. Oh, yeah, the show, right?" I mock with a snap of my fingers. "No, Mom...you're not sharing in that either. All you've done is talk shit and made it hard for me every damn step of the way."

"You are a spoiled bitch," she hisses. "And Brittany is following in your stank ass footsteps."

"Why am I spoiled?" I ask, swinging around to face my Mom. "Because Granny and Papa left me everything? They did it because they knew you would have fucked it all up on your then friends and other stupid bullshit. I would have never benefited from any of it."

"Sure, you benefited. Your gullible ass got knocked up."

"I was raped!" I shriek.

"Yeah, right? Changing your mind after he puts it in isn't rape, girl. Lying about it later to cover it up is-"

"If you weren't my Mom, I would bust you in the face," I growl. "I was raped coming home from the library. I know you were hoping I was throwing leg and spreading it wide, but-"

"It just took you a little longer to embrace that side, huh?"

I clamp my mouth shut, suddenly. "Get the fuck out," I snap. Now," I stress.

She frowns. "I was tired of waiting for a crumb to drop while putting up with your nerdy, ugly girl. Fuck you, Tia. I hope that boy wrecks you up and gives you the clap," she grunts as she strolls from the room.

I'm on her heels. I won't give her the chance to stop my Brit's room to slang her hurtful goodbyes at her. My plan to get Mom out without too much drama fell flat. Her raise voice brought Brit outside of her room anyway. She watches from the step as Mom gets a few things off her chest about me and Brit, her own granddaughter. It was then that I totally forget this was the woman that birthed me but never wanted to care for me. My hand draws back to deliver a stinging slap across her face. I take advantage of her dumfounded reaction to push her out the door.

Panting, I plaster my back onto the front door.

"I'm so sorry," I plead as I look up at the second level.

"It's nothing I didn't know already," mumbles Brit.

I can see through her brave smile. I've seen it enough to know she's hurt.

"I'll stay in tonight. We'll watch Netflicks or a cheesy Hallmark Christmas movie," I suggest while walking towards the stairs.

"No, you aren't. Why are you going to make Granny happy by staying home? That's what she wants. I'm fine. I promise," she replies.

I stop on the landing. I'm torn. I want to go out, but not if it means leaving Brit alone and heart sore. I shake my head.

"Johnny will understand," I remark as I glide by her to walk into my room.

"Ma, please, ...go. I'm fine. I promise."

I narrow my eyes. Why is Brit so pressed for me to leave? She scoops up my heels from the floor to hand them to me.

"I'll wait up to hear all about your date," she beams.

Maybe it's because I'm going out with Johnny. Brit has been over the moon lately. I can only assume it's because her plan for him and I to get together was working.

"Alright," I chuckle. Bending over, I slip on my heels. "I promise not to be out too late. I brought home pizza. It's in the oven."

"Okay! Have fun. Tell Johnny I said, Hi."

A quick hug and we're walking out of my room. I glance over my shoulder at the top of the stairs to watch her heading towards her room. There's a strange smirk on her lips as she reads a text on her cell. I open my mouth to ask her who she's texting with, but then she was gone.

JOHNNY

I'm determined to keep my comments to myself. A person doesn't always want you to fix their problems or tell them what to do. At times, all they want is a listening ear. Besides, I don't want to start talking on this one. Even if Tia and I were dating heavy, I wouldn't touch this one with a ten-foot pole. Speaking against a parent, sibling, or best friend is a danger zone.

All I keep thinking is, 'What a fucking bitch.' I got the feeling from what I heard about Tia's Mom that she was cold-hearted, but never did I think she was like this.

"You got everything alright at home? Didn't your Mom pick Brit up, a lot?"

"You know the games she's been playing, lately. I couldn't count on her, so I've been using a carpooling serves for kids."

I nod. I want to offer to step in, but I also didn't want to make Tia feel as if I'm pushing her or rushing things.

"I think Brit has a boyfriend."

That news doesn't sit well with me. I shift in my chair, take a sip from my glass, and remind myself not to overstep.

"Is that a good thing?"

I try unsuccessfully to keep my voice void of feelings.

"She is in the ninth grade," Tia points out.

"And?"

She tilts her head. "I wanna know who he is."

"Yeah, cuz we already know what he wants," I grumble.

Tia sighs. "I know. I mean, you and I start up, kids at the school finds out, and now she has a guy all up in her face."

"I was thinking the fuck boy wants sex, but that too," I growl. "You have to be careful, though. I'm sure you know not to come off as if a guy could never like her for just her," I warn.

"I know. I know. Maybe, we're off base. I don't think so, but there is a chance."

I pick up the hopefulness in her tone. Yet the expression on her face is as doubtful as mine.

"We'll find out who he is first."

Shit! I used, we. She catches the use of the pronoun, but she doesn't call me on it. Tia nods with a smile. With a wave of my hand, I call for the check.

"I want you home by 10pm. No need to give Brit too much time to invite the son of a bitch over."

My comment causes Tia to freeze. "Maybe that's what the goofy grin on her face was about.

Leaning down, she grabs her purse to fish out her cell.

"Hi Brit, I'm just checking in."

She pauses to listen.

"You don't have cameras in the house?" I whisper.

Tia shakes her head.

"Call me crazy, but um…you don't have anybody over, do you?"

I roll my eyes. What kids admits to their parents they are fucking in their house?

"Yeah, I am used to you not being home alone. Yeah, you're right that I need to get used to you being there alone. Okay, right. Of course, I trust you. You never gave me cause not to. Okay, baby. I'll be back soon. Love you."

Tia wiggles her eyebrows as she puts the cell down on the table. Like I said, I'm going to keep my comments to myself. Stupid, I am not. Brit got herself a little jit, for sure. He might not be at the house, but the asshole is lurking. See the way she played Tia by making Tia feel bad for questioning her. Nah, that's some shit I've pulled to skate around what I was really doing.

"Ready to go? We'll take the beach route to your house," I say.

On the way out, leading Tia by the hand, a few cameras flash.

"Johnny, Johnny want to give a comment? Did you two meet on set? Or were you two already dating?"

I don't respond. A picture is a thousand words. I don't need to add to it. Once in the limo, I roll up the petition, fill our glasses with wine, and entwine my fingers in hers. I smile when she places her head on my shoulder after taking a big sip.

"Congrats on your award nominations."

"Thank you. It's nice having someone not my sister or music fam tell me that."

"You think you'll win?"

Her head moves when I shrug my shoulder. "The producing and collaboration awards, I have a good chance. The Best Rap Song of The Year, not a chance up against those other artists. As for the Album of The Year, not holding my breath, either," I explain.

"Being mentioned is still an honor. It's not like you haven't won others."

"What color is your dress going to be for the awards show?"

My question takes her off guard. She lifts her head to meet my gaze. Tia laughs.

"Well, since it's close to fall, I want a rustic, autumn orange," she jokingly laughs.

I smile. She thinks I'm playing. Yet, I'm already envisioning the cut of the custom made dress draping her body in two weeks. When I walk the red carpet, it will be with Chana and Tia.

"You think we'll win the reality show?" I question, flipping it around on her.

"Even if we don't the producers are going to feature our team heavily, now that you've gotten your way and we're actually doing this."

"Has business picked up?"

"Well, the phone has been ringing. Don't know if the callers are interested in my skills or they are calling for a comment," she answers.

"Just in case you don't know, Yosef and Ryann are back on."

This time, Tia shifts to sit up to face me. I frown at the loss of her body leaning on mine.

"I thought Ryann didn't like being undercover."

"Yosef hasn't told me, but I've heard Ryann's voice through his cell. They're at least talking, which means my boy isn't going to let up till he's back with Ryann."

Tia downs her drink to reach for the bottle for a refill.

"They love each other. I see both sides of the coin, but I would be willing to not go public to keep my relationship safe from prying eyes. This time around, I think Ryann won't push it," she remarks.

Ingesting half of her glass, she licks her lips. "Are you going to sign off on Chana and Richey?"

I sigh as I run my fingers through my hair.

"I'm going to have to fire him."

"No!" exclaims Tia.

"Richey won't come clean while he's employed by me. Me wanting Chana to be happy is more important than Richey having my back. Now, he won't feel like he's fucking the boss' sister to line his pockets. He's been smart with his money while he's been with me. A few years back, I secretly invested in his little brother's restaurant. That place has a waiting list a month deep. When I let Richey go, I've made his brother promise to bring him on as a partner in exchange for my money. As you can see, I've been planning this move for a while."

I'm wondering what was behind Tia look when she leans in to give me a kiss.

"You are so amazing," she whispers. "People have no idea."

"I don't care if people know. All I care about is you knowing who I really am."

I run my thumb over her bottom lip. Suddenly her mouth opens to nibble on the tip. Finishing her drink, she sits the long stem crystal down. Seeing her intentions, I make room for her as she maneuvers to straddle my hips. For a moment, all I do is gaze at her. She is so goddamn breathtaking. In slow motion...or maybe I think she's moving her lips to mine too damn slow, I wait to feel the touch. Once the contact is made, we're gone.

I'll never get enough of this woman. I don't want to get enough. I need everything Tia is, and I want to be a part of everything she's going to be. I use my touch to communicate my feelings. Soft, slow, and intense are my kisses.

"It's too early for that?" She moans into my mouth.

"It's never early when I've been waiting for years to experience it again."

TIA

I should put a stop to this. I should run away. It really is too soon for all of this. Yet, what Johnny is speaking to me in his kiss, in his touch is making me feel all the things I have been secretly longing for. Reaching up, I push the button that cause the roof to retract to allow the night sky above to be seen. Pushing another button causes the moon roof to crack open to let the ocean breeze in. He takes advantage of my craned neck to nibble on my sensitive flesh. This man's, yes, I've come to realize Johnny is far from the boy I thought him to be. His touch is so gentle when he pulls down my dress to expose my breasts.

The tip of his tongue encircles one of my hard nipples. Without taking it into his mouth, he moves to show my other nipple the same type of care. Through cracked eyes, I watch the starry night while he takes me to a new level of desire with just his mouth on my chest.

"I'm gonna pay you back for this afternoon," he whispers while he rubs his rough jaw against my chest.

"Oh, how you plan on doing that? By repeating it, again?"

Shit! How can one man look so damn good. His blue-green eyes hold a sparkle as they open for me to see into his depths. Now, I see why men that are in touch with their feelings make the best musicians. They love without restraint.

"We're taking it slow, tonight," he begins while he gathers my dress to uncover my legs and above. His other hand is at his leather belt.

"There's no need for-"

No doubt he can hear the fear in my tone.

"I just want to see something," he promises.

With a jerk he frees his belt. I don't fight him as he gathers my wrists behind my back to tie in place with his belt.

"Kinky, huh?" I chuckle. "And what are we trying to see?" I tease.

Johnny doesn't immediately answer me. Instead, he keeps me waiting as he leans back. It's as if he's trying to learn me, figure me out, see something that I didn't even know I possessed.

"I want to know if I can make you sing a different tone, express a different emotion."

His voice is deep, low, and electrifying. In minutes, my dress is gone. The warm air caresses my trembling body.

"Ah," he smiles while he opens his pants. "I can make you feel fear. I wonder why?"

"Not fear...excitement," I try to lie.

"I thought we were passed this, Tia."

For the next minute, he does nothing but watch me. In doing nothing, he's making me want him so much. All of this isn't sitting right with me or my rapidly beating heart that's experiencing the strongest pull towards Johnny that I ever have had for a man.

Why won't he fuck me? Why is he watching me like a goddamn hawk? What is the game he's playing?

"No games, Tia."

I freeze with his response.

"Untie me. Take me home," I demand while I try to tilt off his lap.

"No," he snaps.

His word bites, but his actions of straightening me to remain where he placed me are still gentle. Lifting me up, he begins to bring me down on his dick so slowly, I'm left biting my bottom lip to stop my cries. The sensation of the stretching out my pussy is delish, sending shivers up my spine. Back up to his mushroom shape tip to penetrate me deeper until he finally does a death drop to land on his lap.

"Um," is all I can get out.

He slides his hips away from the back of the seat which shoves him further into my womb.

"Take your time," he whispers.

The back of his hand brushes from the side of my face, down my neck, over my collarbone, to cup my breasts. Leaning forward, he licks my neck. The action makes me fall forward.

"Don't be afraid to lean on me. I'll catch you every time, Tia."

He's not talking about now. He's promising so much more. His strong hands grip my ass to maneuver me closer as he grinds into me. In awe, without a single thrust I cum. I don't know if that was the signal Johnny was waiting on, but he finally moves. He creates a slow tempo as he rides the wave of my orgasm. I can't stop trembling. Why am I shaking like a leaf?

"I can feel your heartbeat. Is it my dick that's making it go wild? Or is it me?"

Leaning back, he pins me with is gaze. I move my mouth to speak, but I'm too afraid that my mouth won't say the lies that my mind have conjured up. Suddenly, I feel it. It's a feeling that's so foreign for me. If my hands were free, I would be able to test to prove to myself that it's actually happening. I drop my head, but he's seen. Still moving inside of me with practiced, deep strokes, Johnny forces me to look at him. His lips touch my cheek. The action spreads the clear moisture dampening my skin. Now I know I'm not imagining the tears that fell from wide eyes.

All he does is smile. It's not a cocky grin of "I told you." No, the curves of his lips hold an understanding that hurts to behold. He drops his gaze as if he wants to allow me what's left of my pride. Cuddling me, Johnny nestles my neck, while he supports me with his arms around my waist as he continues to love my body in a way that can only be explained in a song.

I can't believe my reaction to all of this. Maybe it's the pressure of dealing with my Mom. Maybe it's all the years of being Brit's everything, and the weight of the struggle. Maybe it's the fact that for the first time in my life, a man has been able to see the broken woman behind the smile. For the first time, I let the tears flow. I'm not giving, I'm taking. Johnny is filling me up with his strength…and from the intense expression on his face, he's loving every moment.

No words are said. No filthy, fuck me's, no ride this dick's, just the sound of my sobs, our labored breaths, and our moans of pleasure. Once again, my head rolls back to take in the sky. This time, I see a beauty that wasn't there before. It's not like I haven't glanced up at the night sky before. However, when you become so used to seeing the same thing, you stop marveling over it. It's nothing new. Yet, tonight...I'm in awe as I dare to dream of what could be if I'll just let myself go and get out of the way.

Bringing me back, Johnny moves my lips to his to take me higher.

"We're going to make each other feel again, Tia. I'll be good to you, trust me," he breathes into my mouth.

Dear God, I think he means it.

CHAPTER TEN
JOHNNY

"Damn, if my boy ain't back," exclaims the sound guy.

"That's what love can do," adds Yosef from his place on the couch.

I don't even try to deny it. It's true that I've done a complete 360 in the last week since Tia and I started rocking with each other heavy. I'm inspired, back in the studio recording, and I've gotten my golden touchback when it comes to working with the other artists. Not only that, but this record I'm laying down now is taking me back to the days when I would listen to New Edition, Luther, Teddy P, and Marvin Gay on cassette tape. My entire sound is like my first record, that went gold four times. It was an old school vibe that I thought I had lost, but now it's been found.

If Tia wouldn't think me crazy for asking, I would drop to one knee to give her the engagement ring I bought two days ago. Yes, I'm that serious. I guess I have to be happy with giving her the custom silk dress I had made for next week's awards ceremony. I haven't brought it up since the night in the limo. Ryann is working on hair and ensuring his friends have the dress and shoes ready to go. I got jewelry on lockdown by personally selecting the diamonds that will be icing her body.

With three weeks left for taping the reality show, I know Tia's wondering how things are going to be. Right now, we're constantly in each other's faces. Taping in the morning, working on the challenges in the afternoon and into the night, then dinners in the evening, it's easy to cultivate our relationship. Yet, will the effort be made by me to continue on? When I say, I ain't going nowhere, I mean it. If my plan works, I'll be locking Tia down, permanently by December. I'm not risking fucking things up with years of dating. I know what I want.

"I want to lay down the bridge real quick, then we can call it a day," I say from the sound room.

The sound engineer gives me a thumbs up before he begins moving nobs on the soundboard as he gets the playback track ready. My cell in my back pocket vibrates. Smirking, I pull it out. Suddenly, my world tilts, falls to crash and burn. I close my eyes in hopes that what was just texted to me is an imagination of nightmarish proportions. Cracking my eyes, I see that it's not a dream. The pounding on the soundproof window gets my attention. Yosef is shaking his cell in the air while his mouth is moving a mile a minute. I must be in shock because I go back to the image on my cell. The shock doesn't last for long, though.

I'm gonna see if she's just as good as her Mama.

The caption written on the image is the start I needed. I swore to God on the day of my release from jail, years ago, that I was never going to be back behind bars. Well, I'm sorry because I'm going to kill this motherfucker today. The way I head out of the recording booth to enter the main room, everyone knows I'm not in my right mind. Richey was already on his feet by the door leading to the hallway.

"You know where he's at?" I growl.

"I've had people on him for a while," is Richey's answer.

"We're not taking nothing flashy."

He nods as he runs ahead of me to secure a car.

"Are you going to tell Tia?"

Shit, Tia! I can only pray that the school hasn't called her to tell her that Brit isn't there. From my side profile, I see Yosef staring at me when my ringer goes off on my cell. I haven't given Tia a special ringtone, but I know it's her. What happened to the day that the school places the calls at the end of the damn day? I swipe left to send it to voicemail. I got to get in route before talking to her.

"We're ready," announces Richey as I step out of the warehouse onto the street.

Not slowing my steps, he leads us and three others to a black Silverado pickup truck with a cab. It's only enough room for 5.

"I'm going to call Tia. Text me when you get to her. She's at her office. I don't need her doing something crazy. Once I get Brit, I'll bring her home," I inform Yosef.

My friend takes a second to look at the men around me, then he locks gazes with me.

"You're not going down like you did before," promises Yosef.

"It really doesn't matter to me if I do," I admit.

Getting in the passenger seat, I watch through the side door mirror as Yosef takes off running for his car. I don't know if this will be the last time in a long time that I see him as a free man. Reaching up, I open the glove compartment, tug on a pair of leather gloves, and retrieve the gun wrapped up in a worn cloth, All the men on my take know how I do things; clean. Gloves, unmarked guns are the standard. Not that I'm known for doing shady shit, but for those moments when things needed to be handled, I want to be with men that know how to carry things out.

"I called my brother. He's sending our cousins over to clean up whatever mess is made," Richey informs me as he rolls through the security gate and onto the wet, rainy streets. "How did Brit even get picked up by Rafael?"

I scrub my hand down my face in frustration. Times like this, I wish to God I had an Inspector Gadget vehicle.

"I bet it's the boy Brit was fucking around with. I hinted to Tia that she needed to press her about the boy because something just wasn't right, but Tia wanted to be a goddamn friend instead of a parent," I huff. "First Brit said he went to her school. Then she said he kinda did because he took high school and college courses, so he's not on campus all the time. Oh, he works two fuckin jobs so it's going to be hard to get him to come over so we could meet him. Her bullshit stories just kept on changing. The motherfucker is one of Rafael's weak-ass boys."

I glance back down at my cell as the rage overtakes me.

"Don't keep looking at that."

I hear Richey's warning, but I can't turn away. Brit dressed up in a sheer gown, her breast being exposed by someone pulling down the front, and her red shot eyes barely open from whatever she had been given. I can count at least six men crowded around her. I can't stomach looking lower to see the hand between her legs that are being held open by other hands, again.

"Ten more minutes," Richey announces.

I don't know if he thought that info was supposed to calm me. It doesn't. Shit, four guys could have gotten a nut within that time.

This time, when my cell rings, I pick it up.

"Me being here isn't doing a damn thing," admits Yosef.

I can hear yelling and Ryann cursing through the phone.

"Where is Tia? The school called and now–"

"I'm on my way to get her," I say as calmly as I can.

"You? H, how do you know where she is? Why would she call you and not, what the fuck is going on? She skipped school to go where?" she rattles off.

"I'm going to get her," I repeat.

"Where the fuck is she, Johnny! How do you know!" she yells.

I hang up without answering her. I don't want to admit it, but in my heart, I know how this is all going to play out.

Richey underestimated. Not ten minutes but twenty is how long it took for us to turn into the upscale neighborhood. Most of the people were gone with it being 2 pm on a Tuesday afternoon. Those that were home didn't give much thought about the brown skin men pulled to the side of one of the neighborhood roads. In their rich minds, they must be nothing but a group of Mexican gardeners. The SUV with a trailer hitched to the back helped paint the picture. At this point, Richey's cousins only had to fear ICE being called on them to produce Green Cards. Richey passed the SUV, then put our truck into reverse to back up to the trailer.

As soon as I get out, sounds of female laughter and splashing carries over the fence of the fun going on in a back yard of the house two homes down on the right. Seven men pile out of the SUV. Two go to open the back of the trailer to start unloading weed eaters and a blower. The other picks up a large trash bag from the trailer to carry it over to us with his other men following.

"Okay, ya'll got gloves. Here," he tosses me a long sleeve shirt to change into which will cover my arms and neck tattoos.

My watch, necklace, bracelet, ring was left in our truck along with anything else we might be wearing to identify us.

With his gloves now on, he tosses out pairs of cheap-ass tennis shoes that are sized either too small or too big for the casts that the police are sure to take when processing the scene. Lastly, we all get a beanie and one of those plastic Halloween masks from the popup *Halloween Spirits* store. The kind that's strapped around your head by a thin rubber band.

With a jerk of his head, his crew pretending to be lawn men crank up the machines and walk towards the side of the house we're parked in front of. After a few seconds, with our beanies and masks in hand, we follow. Going straight to the back, side gate, we leap over into the next yard. Quickly, we run across the manicured lawn to reach the side gate of the house we're after. We only pause long enough to cover our heads and faces. Hands on the wooden privacy fence, we haul our bodies up and over to land on a patch of grass. It takes a second for the drinking and high partyers playing in the hot sun to even notice we've crashed the event.

Screams fill the air. I don't stop to see what the other men are doing about these people being witness to all this shit. Richey, his cousin and I make a beeline for the inside of the house through the open French Doors. The house is big, but it doesn't have too many rooms. Splitting up, we run through the first floor in no time at all. Meeting by the stairs, we head up.

"Yo, your gun," Richey's cousin points out.

Without hesitation, he switches mine for his, which has a silencer attached to the barrel.

The room wasn't hard to find. There were so many motherfuckers at the scene either to take a turn or to watch, that the door couldn't be closed. Richey takes the lead. He covers the man's mouth closes to us to pull him back into the hallway. I take the man's place to stand in the gap. Cell phones are recording. Brittany is in a half-circle surrounded by four men. Each one has their dicks out. One by one, they are forcing her to suck before the next guy gets her attention with a snatch of her head by her hair for her to repeat on his cock. The sheer cloth, dress, ...I don't know what it is, is hanging around her waist. Her nipples are being pulled on while a guy is on his knees behind her with her ass exposed.

It's too many dicks to count. I just pray that all Brit has is a case of lock jaw, and none of them have had an actual ride. Pushing my way to the side, I lift my gun and shot the guy currently causing the girl to gag in the ass. Instantly, chaos breaks out. There's only one way out, and the three of us got that covered. I'm not here to kill, but these assholes are going to remember this day. Hands up, pleas of help, and for us to stop shooting mix with the screams of pain as we shoot out kneecaps, shins, thighs, arms, and even open hands until one man is left whole and standing.

If Rafael could climb the wall, the rat-faced fucker would. As I move deeper into the room, Richey strolls over to collect Brittany. Even with us hiding our faces, he knows who's here to collect on his wrongdoing.

"I, I...please...d, don't do this. I'm sorry, really. I wasn't going to let it go that far."

As I weave through the maze of the wounded, the closer I get to Rafael, I can tell he's been snorting that shit. In the middle of his begging, I swing with the butt of the gun to lodge it in this mouth. Blood sprays up to cover my jeans. The next hit cracks the side of his head. No longer is he able to plead with coherent words. His mouth moves, but nothing but wheezes of air and grunts are passing through his thin lips. He might be brain dead, maybe not. Frankly, I don't care. Stepping back, I level the gun at his head.

Richey coughs a warning. My hand shakes with the desire to explode this fucker's brain matter all over the wall.

Richey coughs, again.

I hold up my gloved hand to let him know I understand. Repositioning the gun, I shoot Rafael in the next best location. He might have been unable to figure out what day of the week it was after the hit to the head. A bullet to his dick brought him back. I've never heard a person squeal like a pig before. Even from all the beatings and tortures I've carved out in the past, my ears had never heard such a high pitch of pure pain before.

Nice and clean, with only the people we wanted to hit being affected. Just the way I like it. Yet, this was just the beginning for Rafael. Not only is he going to be dick less but he's also going to be a broke, homeless, cast out, ugly motherfucker once I'm finished.

TIA

I was at the door the second I heard the knob turning. I'll never forget the sight of a swaying Brittany, hair a mess, draped in a large sweatshirt and sweatpants clinging to Johnny as a lifeline. Rushing to her side, she shrinks away to bury her face in his chest. Her reaction is like a slap in the face.

"I don't want to see her. Don't let her see me like this," begs Brit.

"Is she drunk? Where are her clothes?" I demand to know. "Where were you?" I ask as I jerk on her arm, forcing her to lift her head to look at me.

I make a wide turn to look from Ryann to Yosef, to Richey, to a man I've never seen, then back to Johnny with his stone face expression.

"All ya'll get the fuck out. I'll figure this out myself," I order. Going to the door, I open it wide, yet no one is moving.

"Please, Johnny...d, don't leave me with her. S, she'll beat me. I, I know it," stammers Brit.

Angry, I slam the door, rattling the front windows.

"Damn right I'm going to beat your ass!" I yell. "Every second that passes you're pissing me off," I spit.

Johnny closes his eyes as he pushes Brittany away. The look he gives her is one mixed with disappointment and rage.

"She skipped school to go to a party with that boy she's been fucking around with," Johnny speaks at last.

The amount of air that leaves my lungs also leaves me lightheaded. Covering my mouth with my hand, I lower my head to glance at the floor as I steady my other hand on my hip.

"What happened?" I question in a muffled tone.

Johnny takes a breath to speak, but I raise my hand for him to give me a second to get ready. I know this answer is going to take me out. Instead of Johnny's voice, it's Brit's.

"Wanna know what happened? I was set up. I'm the dumb girl looking for some action only to get played by a guy that was paid to talk to me."

"Paid," I repeat, weakly. "Why would...was this a prank by those bitches at your school?"

"They," she starts in a husky voice as she begins to cry. "They, they..."

"Jesus, no," I cry as I take a step towards her.

Once again, she chooses to use Johnny as a shield by hiding behind him.

"I need to brush my teeth and a bath," she cries.

"No, no, no...I, I, did they, please not-"

"We got there in time before any physical damage, but other acts were done," Johnny remarks, slowly to ensure I understand.

I nod. Hearing that doesn't make it any better, but it's something.

"How did you know where to find her? Did you call him?" I press.

"Not a call, a text," he pauses, "from Rafael showing me what he was planning to do."

I must have blacked out on my feet because all I can do is look at Johnny. I see Brit stop hiding behind him to say something to me. I tilt my head in hopes to make my hearing turn back on, but it's not working. Now Ryann is in the frame. He's talking, too.

"Get out."

Was that me that said that? Heads are looking in my direction, so yes. I must have spoken the two words.

"Get out," I repeat, firmer this time.

Johnny is moving for the door only for Brittany to grab hold to him.

"Why mama? It's all my fault, not his. He's not the one that told me to skip. He was the one that tried to warn me about the boy in the first place, but I wouldn't listen. Please!"

Johnny snatches his hand from hers. Brit has a hurt expression on her face, but she reaches out for him again.

"Don't be mad at me, please, Johnny. I'm so sorry. I messed everything up," glancing over at me, "Mama, don't do this. I don't want him hurt because of me," she cries as she fights to keep him from reaching the door.

"It is his fault," I snap. "You got caught up in this shit because of his friend. So, the man couldn't mess with me, so he fucked around with you, instead," I point out.

"But, but,...no Johnny, wait, WAIT!" screams Brittany.

Richey, and the guy I've never seen before files out after him. Brittany screams while she pulls at her braided hair.

"It's all my fault. Why you got to do this, Mama? He saved me. He warned me. All you did was believe all my lies. If it weren't for Johnny they would have...I'm never gonna forgive myself," she cries as she takes off for the stairs.

I make a swipe at her to stop her, but she slips through my fingertips.

"Give her some time," suggests Yosef.

"I can't do that. She might-"

"I'm going with her," offers Ryann while he jogs up the stairs. I'm sure he shares my worries of Brittany cutting herself to the point of injury or God forbid death.

I'm at a loss. I don't know how many turns in a circle I make. On my last rotation, Yosef shoves a glass of wine in my hand. Without hesitation, I toss it back to snatch the bottle out his hand.

"My baby," I cry while I stumble into the living room. "I can't believe-"

"Johnny got there before the worse could happen."

"Why ya'll keep saying that?" I yell. "Nothing should have happened at all. She should have never been there in the first place."

"Kids do stupid things, Tia. You know that."

"Yeah, kids do, but Brittany wasn't one of those kids. She never, never did anything like this before until he gave in the picture," I replied, hotly.

Yosef gets to his feet. "So, you just gonna leave it like that, huh? You're gonna put all the damn blame on Johnny instead of taking your slice. It's sad when a fifteen-year-old girl is smarter than her mom. At least, Brit is upstairs feeling guilty over what she did, but your dumbass won't face the truth."

"Alright," I hiss, slamming the bottle down, "what's my truth?" I sneer.

"That you've listened so much to your wack-a-doodle mom to the point that you can't think for yourself when it comes to Brit. You actually believed the obvious bullshit she was feeding you about that boy? I mean, even I was looking side-eyed, but you're so used to your Mom putting her two cents in, telling you what to do, that you let that girl dupe you. Even when you could see that your old lady was undercutting you, you still would go along with it. Me, Ryann, hell Johnny, we all could see it. The girl has issues. She needs help," he stresses in a low voice.

"You can go, too."

"Yeah, yeah, I'll go so I don't have to be here when you call your Mom over so you can eat her shit. I mean, we all know that's what you're going to do because you feel like you need her help. It's like you're a verbally abused person that keeps going back to get beat again when you don't have to because you have others that care...the right way."

"You got a lot of advice for somebody too afraid of being clowned for being gay," I sass.

Yosef freezes. "At least, I'm not blind. You hear that sound? Welcome to your life, Tia."

**

The reality show went to hell in a handbasket. The lead our team had slipped due to us not being about to complete the challenges on time. Yosef, Ryann, and I limped along, but the tension among us made it, so we didn't sync well. Chana made an excuse that Johnny was busy with record label obligations which kept them away from the set. Luckily, the producers had enough film including Johnny and me to make the season juicy enough to get the viewers. In the end, our team came in the final three.

Now that we were free from taping, I'm back at the office. Unlike what Yosef claimed, no that's a lie. He seemed to have read my mind. I was going to go to grovel at my Mom's feet for her to come back. However, I decided to forge it alone. I mean, there was never nothing stopping me from taking Brittany to school. I didn't do it because Mom was here. Hell, I make my own hours. I really didn't need her to pick Brit up, or to cook, or to be home with her. All of those things I could and am doing now. All it took was me actually putting to use my home office on the first floor.

I just wish fixing things between Brittany, and I was that easy. She still isn't talking to me after a week. Every day she asks me to call Johnny so she can apologize, but I refuse. No longer is she the happy student whose cares had been finally put to rest. She's retreated back into her shell. The only contact I've had with Johnny came with a knock on the door.

"Tia?"

I examine the woman standing in my doorway.

"Yes."

"May I come in?"

Stepping to the side, I let her enter. By the time I close the door, she's fished out a crisp business card with golden, embossed writing.

"I'm here on retainer from Mr. Thicke. He believes you and your daughter are in need of my services. Can we speak for a moment?"

She doesn't wait for my welcome. Instead, she glides silently into the living room to take a seat.

"Is Brittany here?"

"Um, I didn't consent to anything."

She shrugs her boney shoulders. "Either you speak with me, or you can speak with a not so nice rep from child services after I report what happened to Brittany last week," she smirks. "Why don't you call her down?"

"This is blackmail?"

"Is it? I am here to give you and your daughter much-needed therapy."

I open my mouth to respond.

"Did Johnny really send you?"

The woman stands to face Brittany leaning in the archway.

"He did, and he's footing the bill, so I'm here to help you," she smiles. "Well, will you join us?" she asks as she gestures to the empty couch.

With a nod, Brit walks into the room. Two sessions in, Brit only talks to me during those meetings. Other than that, she's silent, or she gives me one-word answers.

I should be happy that the reality show and yes, being connected to Johnny for that short time has paid off. He's even personally sent business my way. Clients are booking my services, and it's all because of him. Wish I had the guts to tell him all about my good fortune. That day, standing in my foyer is on replay on a daily bases. With hindsight, I see I was wrong to place the entire blame at his feet. I jumped to conclusions to assume the worse about him, clearing all the times he's proven to me that I was so very, very wrong about him.

He's gone out of his way to not cross my path. No, he hasn't come out to announce his fling with me is over. I know he never would. The press and public will get the hint to move on to the next hot topic. I'm sure once the show airs, there will be moments of awkwardness, but I'm determined to handle it.

Now, this is my life. Yosef called it. As I sit on the couch with a glass of wine in my hand, silence is my constant companion. The chill of the turning weather outside seems to seep into the room to make me even more aware that I am alone. I take a sip and steal a glimpse of the remote sitting on the coffee table.

Tonight is the night of the awards show. My hand itches to scoop it up to catch some of the red carpet pre-show coverage. It hovers over the piece of rectangular plastic. Suddenly, I snatch it away due to the knocking on the door. Fumbling to the door, I'm greeted by a delivery woman.

"Hello, I have a package for this address."

"Um, okay," I mumble as I take the electronic pad to sign.

Before I can close the door, Ryann pulls up on the street. The doors on his white Lexus opens.

"You haven't bathed," he shouts up to me.

"No, it's too early to take a shower," I frown.

He strolls around the car to stand at the foot of the steps. His bag toting friends exchange looks.

"The awards ceremony is tonight," he points out.

"And?"

With a scoff, he climbs the stairs to shove me back inside.

"Bitch don't tell me we did all this work for no shout out," complains Bianca in his deep voice.

"Shut up," hisses Ryann. He sighs, "Johnny was going to take you to the awards show. He had me make your wig, and Bianca and his team did your dress and shoes. Those must be the diamonds Johnny bought for you."

I drop the package as if I had been burned. From where I don't know, Brit appears to bend down to pick up the package. I have no words. All I can do is follow her into the living room as she rips through the shipping tape to open the box.

"Wow!" she exclaims.

I'm too scared to walk behind her to take a look. The others don't share my fear. I watch their expressions as the open box comes into few.

"That's custom, honey," remarks the tall, thin, white guy on Bianca's glam squad with a sugary snap of his fingers.

It becomes obvious I'm not moving. Brit slowly turns the red velvet case for me to see. Slack-jawed. I'm completely slack-jawed. Teardrop and emerald-cut diamonds are positioned to create an oval leaf pattern all set in gold. At the end is an off-centered, large teardrop cut yellow diamond.

"Actually, it's a replica of the Wallace Chan 200million masterpiece. It's a total weight of 637 carats. The brownish, yellow diamond pendent is over 407 carats all by itself. Johnny showed me a picture of the original before he had it remade for you to make sure it would match this."

On his cue, Bianca's friend pulls down the zipper of the garment bag in his hand to reveal a breathtaking silk dress in the autumn, rustic orange I had teased him about. It wasn't that much of a showstopper when it came to gowns. It was made for my body with one shoulder, a high split up the thigh, and a nice dip to show off the diamonds going around my neck.

"Th, that, this is too much," I point with a shaky finger.

"Let's get it poppin', Cinderella," smacks Bianca.

"Shit, I'm not going," I cry.

"See, I told you I was going to show the fuck out if this didn't happen," growls Bianca.

"Mama, you have to go," wails Brit. "All the money Johnny spent."

"I'll pay you back for the wig and clothes, and that box is going back to him, so, he's not out of nothing," I reply in a rush.

"I knew this was going to happen," mumbles Ryann.

"You are so dumb," hisses Brit as she plops down in a chair.

She better not be cussing under her breath while she switches on the TV. Like a moth to the flames, we're all in a trance by the coverage of the awards show. A late-night show celebrity is hosting the event. The star-studded guest all laugh at a joke that is kinda funny. My eyes scan the beautiful people in hopes of a glimpse of Johnny in the crowd. I come up short though. I can hear Ryann and his friend arguing while I continue to watch and hold my breath. All I have to do is wait for one of the categories he's nominated for. The camera is sure to pan to him.

What if he replaced me with another date?

I close my eyes over the possibility that I might come face to screen with the woman he's moved on to. I mean, just because I'm still heart sore and processing the break up doesn't mean he's in the same boat as me. Time goes by. More jokes, more presenters, a few commercial breaks and performances, but no Johnny.

"Now, the category of Best Rap Collaboration."

My ears perk up. I scoot to the edge of the couch as if I'm getting ready to jump through the mounted 32-inch flat-screen. One by one, the faces of the rappers in the crowd are added to a square panel. Suddenly, I suck all the air out of the room at the sight of Johnny. Chana is to his right and to his left is an empty seat. Relief and sadness washes over me. I could have been sitting there. I could have been the one holding his hand as we waited to hear the presenters call the winners names. My Lord he looks good, better than the last time I've seen him. His chiseled jaw is sporting a nice 5 o'clock shadow. The longer portion of his hair on top is brushed back from his forehead. His face is expressionless. He looks flawless and spills of sex and authority in his tailored black suit with crisp white shirt and black bow tie.

"And the winners are."

Johnny leans over to listen to Chana whisper something in his ear.

"Johnny Thicke and Nas; Break Every Rule."

His eyebrow arching is the only sign of shock to register on his face. I follow his tattooed hands when he buttons his suit jacket as he stands. Along the way towards the stage, others pat him on the back. Near the front, Nas joins him to walk up the steps to reach the mic. He smiles at the presenter, then turns to take one of the two trophies out of the hands of the females along the side. Quickly, he steps to Nas, whispers something, and Nas nods, giving Johnny first crack at the mic.

"Thank you," he begins. "This speech is going to be a bit different, so bear with me. I had been actually marking off the days until tonight, not because I was hoping to win one of these, but because I was going to be bringing a very special woman with me to the event. Unfortunately, if you were to check, you'll see that her seat is empty," he stops as if he's looking at the empty seat. "I promised myself that if I won, I wasn't going to use the time to praise people that I can talk to later, but to try to get through to the person that's not only missing from that seat, but the woman that's wrecking my every day because she's missing from my life.

He pauses as Nas pats him on the back for encouragement. The camera spans the crowd to show the moved expressions on the faces of the other guests. A few even shouts for him to go on.

"I've made millions and a name off of singing about love and relationships, but not till I met Tia did I join the millions of people that have actually experienced love. It's so funny how I could make people find love, and feel it, but I've spent most of my career longing for it. Needless to say, forces that didn't want me happy has fucked things up. In spite of her treating me like shit instead of listening and talking to me, the days without her is too much to bear, so I can't just walk away. Ya'll say I'm the white man with the Luther Vandross voice, so let's see."

"Oh shit, he's going to sing Luther," shouts Ryann. "It's over! It's fuckin' over!"

By the time Johnny parts his lips to start, he's nothing but a watery image. Hands clutching my chest, I listen in disbelief.

"I wanna tell you baby, the changes I've been going through, missing you. Till you come back to me. I don't know what I'm going to do."

The crowd is losing their minds over his singing. Women are actually crying as they stand to their feet, hands waving in the air wildly. Men are smirking while telling him to sing.

"Don't you remember you told me you love me, baby. You said you'll be coming back this way again."

Nas at his side is nodding his approval while the two female presenters look as if they are debating fucking Johnny on the stage in front of millions.

Baby, baby, baby, baby, oh Tia, Baby...I love you. I really do," he sings in his soulful, honey voice. With a nod, "Thank You," he finishes before he walks away with a standing ovation.

"Tia, where are you, gurl? Whatever happened, after all of that... He sung Luther's *Superstar*, for Christ sakes," the host cries.

"I need to get ready," I announce.

CHAPTER ELEVEN
JOHNNY

My heart is heavy. I went through the rest of the awards show praying, hoping for Tia to appear, but nothing. She didn't even text or call me. Of course, she might not have caught my speech, but I know Ryann or someone had to have shown her by now.

"I'm doing this press, then I'm leaving," I inform Chana while we're led to a large open room with many interviewing stations. I stroll by a few celebrities that are sharing their excitement of winning. A few stop to pat me on the shoulder as they tell me not to give up on love.

"When he's done, it will be your turn, Mr. Thicke."

I nod while I plaster my shoulder to the wall to wait. A chill runs up my spine. A heat that I haven't felt in a while tickles the hairs on the back of my neck. Slowly, I turn. My world stops. Widen eyed, I root myself in place to keep from falling on my ass. Chana turns worried to figure what's come over me. It doesn't matter that the room is filled. I only see the slow approach of one woman. I'm dumbstruck by the effortless, amazing grace and stunning beauty of Tia. My greedy eyes eat up every inch of her from her hair to her firm breast, full hips, to her exposed shapely thigh to finish at the tips of her shoes, only to start the process, again.

My heart contracts. I know she's coming, but she's not moving fast enough for me. I need to hold her, touch her, kiss her to prove to myself that this isn't a dream. I hope Chana caught the trophies I push on her to free up my hands. My long strives weave me through the people. In no time, I'm towering over Tia. Taking a deep breath, I inhale her scent as I fight to control the beating of my heart.

"Tia," I whisper in a gravelly voice.

I raise my hand to touch her, then pull back. I'm unsure of what I should do. Suddenly the lack of noise and movement registers. A quick glance over her head shows me that all eyes, cell phones, lights, and camera are focused on us.

"I came for the rest of the concert."

Her comment causes me to lock gazes with her again. I open my mouth, then she moves.

"I was hoping for a private concert," she adds.

I close my mouth. I freeze as her hand gravitates towards my face. I can't stop my eyes from going hooded as I turn my face to fit in the cup of her hand.

"I, I think I love you," she whispers on a broken breath.

I have no words to respond. My hand snakes around her waist to pull Tia in my embrace. I marvel over how perfect she fits at my side as if it was my rib that was taken to create her with the dust and clay of the earth. All I know is that I'll never forget the way she tastes or the way she makes me feel as I pour my soul into this kiss. In my mind, I find myself praying that it will brand her, bind her to me forever.

"I left the ring at home, but will you marry me?" I pant against her parted lips.

I don't blink as I read her face. There's no fear in the depths of her eyes.

"First the ring, then you'll get my, yes."

The smile that creeps on my face is damn near cracking it. Tossing back my head, I laugh. Without a wave goodbye, I began to drag Tia from the room with the sounds of cheers at our backs. I'm already setting the date for the wedding two months from today. Our first child will be conceived on our honeymoon. Finally, the man that's claimed to have it all actually does have it all.

THE END

Hello Readers!

I had so much fun writing this book to the point that it wrote itself. My love for the classic R&B was the soundtrack and my love for Jon B…and a bit of Robin Thicke did the rest. Of course, I had to tat up my version of the singer and make him a bad boy with a big heart. In this book, I touched on a lot of issues. Keeping toxic people around just because they are blood or because you share a history. The fact that it's alright to move on from people that refuse to grow, yet they want to leech off your success or talents. It's alright to seek professional or spiritual help to heal to ensure you are ready for the future, and also, the struggles many people are facing when dealing with their sexuality.

I think I can list out more things, but seeing how you just read the book, I'm sure you got the little messages of hope, strength, and love that I laced into the lives of these characters.

As always, thank you for all the support, leaving a review, for sharing the link, telling your friends, and for just being the awesome readers that you are. Most of all, THANK YOU for enjoying what I so love to do, which is creating one love story at a time. SO, what's next? I think it's time for the New York Detective, Kegan McCormac and his now wife, Moneà to entertain us for the rest of 2019.

Till Then, Peeps…

Christine Gray

Keep In Touch!
https://www.christinesappgrayauthor.com

Looking for a publishing home?

After Hours Publications, is accepting submissions from motivated, talented Authors Experienced and NON- Experienced with a knack of creating drama filled, romantic, downright sappy stories desired. SHORT STORIES with a min of 18k words, also welcomed.

If you are a lover of Interracial Romance, AHP is the publishing house for you; Contemporary, Paranormal, Historical, New Adult Romance. Interested? Submit the first 3-4 chapters with your synopsis to Submissions@afterhourspublications.com.

Check out our website for more information:

www.afterhourspublications.com

Be sure to LIKE our After Hours Publications page on Facebook.

CPSIA information can be obtained
at www.ICGtesting.com
Printed in the USA
LVHW042110211119
638113LV00006B/1181/P

9 781695 400610